FULL SPEED TO HEAVEN

Published by Sapere Books.

24 Trafalgar Road, Ilkley, LS29 8HH

saperebooks.com

ISBN: 978-0-85495-075-1

FOREWORD

This is the story of men trapped by a freak series of 'flash' hurricanes, one spawning the other so swiftly that they became one gigantic storm — the worst in living memory. Those who sailed in the northern latitudes of the Atlantic in the winter of 1942-3 still recall with lingering awe the savage fury of that turbulent world few so seldom see and fewer survive. That it happened against a background of war is incidental; it could happen again in those ice-strewn, bitter seas.

The hurricane is my villain; the veteran American-built Canadian destroyer *Concord* is my hero. For twenty-five days and nights she was thrashed by monstrous waves, whipped by a shrieking wind and weighed down by the heavy ice formations which threatened to capsize her.

Like her officers and men — Louis Strong, John Masefield, Peter Boland, Bill Gridley and the rest — a few hundred sailed into that hell without relief. Those who returned were not unscathed; they came back mentally bruised by the horror of what they had seen.

The experiences endured by *Concord* are based on real-life events, but the men are fictitious. The crew are a mixture of British and Canadian; the officers are British except the Captain, Lieutenant-Commander Louis Strong, R.C.N.R., a French-Canadian. Through him, this book is largely a tribute to the Royal Canadian Navy, many officers of which I have known, admired and respected.

TERENCE ROBERTSON

Toronto

1

Concord slid easily through the swell of the North Channel. Beneath an impenetrable overcast, a northeast wind, moderate in all but its biting chill, flicked foam from the crests of a slightly running sea. A grey day — grey sky, grey sea, grey ships.

Forty merchantmen wallowed fitfully into convoy formation, harried by the insistent manoeuvres of the patient escorts. By late afternoon the tedious shepherding was done and the convoy headed for the open Atlantic at eight knots in six long columns. *Firefly,* the escort leader, lay well up ahead, zig-zagging across the line of advance. Two corvettes guarded each side of the convoy while *Concord* crossed and re-crossed the rear of the columns.

There was nothing impressive about the escort; nothing in numbers or appearance to inspire confidence or offer comfort to the merchant crews who now approached the start line for their dash through the U-boat blockade. But appearances meant little in that protracted, relentless war at sea. The six tiny warships looked as puny as David, yet Goliath could throw down his challenge and be met by the six acting as one, sweeping into action under the guiding hand of their leader. No signals, no fuss, no frantic jamming of the R/T with requests for instructions, just one smooth machine drilled and trained to a pitch where few situations could arise in which each ship would not know exactly what was expected of her.

The 5th Escort Group had acquired a reputation for protecting convoys and sinking U-boats which was better than most and justified the respect of other groups. For this reason the Convoy Commodore, sailing in the leading ship of the centre column, signalled to *Firefly*: 'Glad to have you along. We are flattered to have the 5th E.G. in attendance.'

On *Concord*'s bridge, the Yeoman of Signals gazed intently through his telescope to intercept *Firefly*'s reply. Even before the leader's signal lamp — more than eight miles away — had finished spelling out each word, he was calling it out to Strong.

'*Firefly* calling Commodore, sir. Begins: "From Frankie to Johnnie..."' Those of the bridge personnel within hearing began to snigger. The leader's tendency to cover his most pertinent signals with a veneer of humour was well known. '"We share the same bed. Keep well tucked up at nights."'

This reference to the habit of merchantmen in convoy to straggle amused Lieutenant-Commander Louis Strong, R.G.N.R., who, muffled in duffel coat and sweaters, sat hunched on a hard wooden seat behind the glass windscreens on the front of the bridge. John Masefield stood to his left, near the asdic operator.

'I bet there isn't one skipper in that lot,' said Strong, 'who wouldn't prefer to take his own chances and sail alone. Most of these chaps think that convoys attract the U-boats whereas a single ship sailing independently might slip through undetected.'

Masefield eyed one laggard through his binoculars. 'There's one now, sir. He's going to straggle in the hope we leave him behind to find his own way. Shall we hoist the hunting flag and drop a depth charge under his stern, sir? That might scare him into formation.'

Strong grinned. 'Too early for that sort of thing, Number One.'

On the port side of the bridge Peter Boland searched southwards, looking for points of land on which he could take bearings. He turned to Strong. 'And what would you do if you were still in the Merchant Service, sir?'

His eyes flicked towards the Captain coolly. His taunt was scarcely hidden. By reminding Strong that he was just another temporary naval officer, Boland was trying to reduce the rank gap and retaliate for the lecture he had been given yesterday.

Strong ignored both the remark and the Navigator. 'Number One, I've got some reports to clear up. Let me know when the convoy makes its dusk alteration of course.'

'Aye, aye, sir.'

He left the bridge and Masefield turned on the Navigator. 'That was a damn silly thing to say, Peter. The Old Man isn't going to like that sort of thing and you know it.'

Boland chuckled and stepped on to the compass dais beside the First Lieutenant. After lighting a cigarette, he said casually, 'Don't take life so seriously, Number One. The Old Man needs reminding that a change of clothes doesn't change the man.'

Masefield looked at the Navigator with troubled eyes. 'Look, Peter, for heaven's sake forget the blasting he gave you yesterday. It was probably for your own good anyway. We can't afford to have long-drawn-out grudge rows between ourselves, let alone involve the Captain. He's got enough to worry about without having you on his neck the whole time.'

Boland's smile was without humour. 'It's all very well for you, John. You've got a honey of a wife to go home to. Now I was just getting along fine with that little Wren in Captain D's office when the Old Man interfered. Last night would have ended in complete surrender. He put paid to all that…'

Masefield was already looking away, trying to hide the misery he was sure would show. 'Don't be so bloody silly, Pilot,' he muttered vehemently. 'You can't carry on a vendetta against the Captain just because of some girl in uniform.'

He could not disguise the bitterness in his voice. Boland glanced at him in vindictive, curious silence. Then he asked quietly, 'Just why did you come back from your leave, John? You know, I don't believe Sonia was working away somewhere—'

'I don't give a damn what you think,' Masefield interrupted savagely. 'For Christ's sake, shut up.'

Boland went on as though the First Lieutenant had not spoken. 'No, if she had been away you could have joined her. No, that's not it. What did happen, John? Come on, old boy, if there's trouble between you two lovebirds, let Uncle Peter help you sort it out.'

The First Lieutenant hid his eyes behind the binoculars. A futile gesture; they brought into sharp focus that nightmare scene in London, in the bedroom…

Lieutenant John Masefield, R.N., jerked awake as the Liverpool-London night express jolted to a stop. He blinked for a moment to clear the sticky tissues of his eyes and peered sleepily over his left shoulder at the black-painted compartment window. Some of the paint had been scraped off by previous inquisitive passengers, and if he looked hard enough through the bare sliver of glass he could see searchlights chasing engine noises across the sky.

Another air-raid warning; another wait.

He leaned back in his seat, attempted vainly to stifle a yawn, and tried to increase the space between the side of the compartment and his neighbour by pronounced shrugging of his shoulders. He succeeded in persuading the large body on his right to move slightly away, and, feeling maliciously elated at this silent victory, he squinted distastefully into the gloom. Long ago, someone had removed the blue blackout bulbs so that to any one passenger the rest remained anonymous, indistinguishable.

An elbow nudged hard at his right side and a gust of breath, combining the stink of alcohol with the bad odour of cheap tobacco, blew heavily on his cheek. The voice that went with it was hoarse and fruity; it bellowed, although quite obviously intending to whisper.

''Ere, chum, 'ave a drop of this. Just the job.'

Masefield tried to remember which of the many large shapes that had fought their way into the compartment at the last stop had sat beside him. He decided it must be the one who might be a Petty Officer.

'Thanks, I think I will.' He forced an edge of humour into his normally firm, incisive voice. 'The L.M.S. Service isn't what it used to be. The war, I suppose.'

He groped for the bottle thrust at him, praying that it should be Scotch or beer and fearful that it might be cold tea, the beverage most wives gave their sailor husbands about to embark on long train journeys. The bottle tipped and raw rum tore away the parchment in his mouth, burned his throat and left a cloying sweetness behind that made him thirstier than ever. His face twisted in unseen revulsion as he handed back the bottle and gasped, 'Good grief, I hate that stuff!'

The reply was a gurgling chuckle that reverberated through the darkness. 'Never mind, chum. Ruddy good stuff, that. Nothin' better than Nelson's Blood on a night like this.' Then the hearty rum donor thumped a huge hand on the arm of his neighbour on the other side. 'Your turn, matey. 'Ave a good swig. Keeps away the germs and puts you nicely to sleep.'

The echoes of the gale died away and Masefield huddled lower in his corner seat attempting to stretch his legs, a manoeuvre blocked by someone else's. He gave the offending feet a sharp jab with the point of his shoe and was rewarded with a startled grunt opposite him. With the obstacles removed, Masefield stretched luxuriously and closed his eyes with an expression of smug satisfaction, ignoring the chain reaction of unscrambling legs he had set off. In the middle of this readjustment of positions the train shuddered briefly, and then, with considerable clanging and more jolting, it resumed the journey southwards.

He thought of Sonia, the lovely blonde Sonia, who almost a year ago had become his wife. He imagined her standing at Euston early in the morning to meet him, but drowsily remembered this could not be so. There had been no time to wire her, and he had not had the right change for a telephone call; anyway, it was an unearthly hour to expect anyone to get up and wait on a cold platform.

She would be in bed when he arrived. *That's nice,* he thought contentedly, *just where she should be to welcome home her seldom-seen husband.* It had been a long time since his last leave, the only one in their marriage. God knew, it had been short enough. In fact, since the wedding, they had not been together for as many days as a decent honeymoon deserved.

Good heavens, who was that idiot lighting a cigarette? The compartment was filled with smoke already, and acrid fumes mingled with the faintest suggestion of sweat. Although it was November the compartment was stuffy, even warm, and Masefield knew without looking that the heater handle was over to cold while hot steam was surging through the heater pipes. Bloody trains! First thing he would need when he got home would be a bath — well, no, not really. The bath could wait.

The express crawled into Euston shortly before six in the morning. It was dark and the shaded station lights glowed bleakly through the frosty air. Masefield shuddered inside his greatcoat and remembered the date. November 15, his brother's birthday. Dear old Aubrey, an unemotional fish as cold as the day on which he was born. This would make Aubrey twenty-nine, just eighteen months older than himself. *We're both getting old already,* thought Masefield, *older than our years because of those blasted politicians who get the country into trouble and then expect the Masefields of the world to unscramble it all.*

He smiled reflectively. Why should he really complain? That's what he was paid for. And after all, it was a pretty good life in peacetime.

On the platform, the burly Petty Officer who had been so generous with his rum glanced at Masefield's stripes with obvious embarrassment. 'Sorry, sir.' A dozen passengers two coaches away looked round, startled, as the boom echoed round the cavernous station. 'Couldn't see your rank in that bloomin' blackout.'

Masefield grinned amiably. 'That's all right. But for heaven's sake bring beer with you next time.'

'Aye, aye, sir.' The Petty Officer beamed, boomed again and saluted as Masefield turned away and strode off towards the ticket gate, his twenty-seven years carried lightly on square, well-set shoulders and the canvas holdall swinging jauntily in his hand. The war had already receded, and the image of Sonia danced tantalizingly before his eyes. She was a ballet dancer, acclaimed by London's balletomanes as a coming prima ballerina. He had seen her dance a hundred times, scintillating from the corps de ballet and in the few minor solos carefully chosen for her by a critical choreographer. At sea — or, for that matter, anywhere away from her — he could switch his thoughts to Sadler's Wells and see her dancing for him alone.

The taxi queue was beginning to blossom, but the fifth cab was his. He threw his holdall in the back seat, climbed in beside it and called out, 'St Ives Court, Marble Arch.'

The cabby nodded and shouted at the queue, 'Anyone else for Marble Arch direction?' There were no takers, and thankfully Masefield settled back to concentrate once more on his wife, who was really still a bride.

She would be curled up in that big four-poster bed they had rescued from the bargain basement at Maples. She had looked quite gorgeous that day, he decided, dressed in a figure-hugging tan suit and high-heeled suede sandals with the latest ankle straps, and her brilliant blonde hair gleaming in the sunlight. When they had seen the bed her eyes had sparkled mischievously as she demanded it, complete with canopy and curtains.

'It's too divine, John. Of course we must have it. I've always wanted to — well, you know what — in a four-poster. Let's find out how much the man wants for it.'

So John had written a cheque and they had rushed back to the small flat to prepare for the triumphal entry. Funny thing about that bed: Sonia had never been able to use it for the purpose she had demurely implied. The slightest movement set it rocking and screeching like an outraged hen. No matter what they did, it defied all their attempts to reduce the noise.

On their first night in the flat, romance had struggled vainly against the bed until eventually Sonia had refused to make love in it. She had whispered, 'No, darling, the whole block will hear us and know what we're doing. I couldn't bear that. Let's just sleep in the thing, it's too passion-killing for anything else. We can use some pillows on the floor.' And with a low chuckle she had tossed her two pillows on the carpet and leapt from the bed, her slender body silhouetted momentarily against the grey square of window.

Now she would be alone in that great bed, naked because she hated nighties or pyjamas. The long waves of her thick fair hair, always pulled tightly to her head when she danced, would be tumbled loosely about her shoulders. Her large blue eyes, that sometimes became violet pools and often changed again to laughing grey, would be hidden in sleep; they would reveal themselves only when he walked into the bedroom as though part of her dream. The thought pleased him, and he wondered vaguely if she dreamt of him often, even at all.

The taxi turned into Edgware Road and his expression changed as the first doubts sprang into focus. Recently her letters had become filled with odd references to late nights, long rehearsals and boring parties. There had been hints that he was staying away too long, and more than one letter had been cut short on the excuse that she was suffering from constant headaches. He had replied with an anxious enquiry as to whether she was wise to work so hard and stay out late at nights, but there had been no reply to this and her letters had become less frequent.

He had asked her to write more often and her answer had been curt, almost hysterically so. It was all right for him to talk, but did he realize how boring London could be when a girl was married and had to live alone? Did he begrudge her a little fun sometimes so that she could relax? She was still young, only twenty-two, and in any case most of the parties involved theatre people. Even if there was a war on, she still had her career to think about and know the right people. That was important because she wanted to try film work. Furthermore, she was worried about the call-up, which might mean being sent to a factory or into some service. There was a way out which lots of women were employing: she must have a baby, because expectant mothers were never called up.

By the time the taxi stopped outside the small modern block, Masefield had the door open and change in his hand. 'How much?'

'Well, guv'nor, there's three bob on the clock, but what with air raids and suchlike, I ain't made only a few bob, and bin up all night too. We cabbies who stay out late these nights don't get much, I'll tell yer.'

Masefield thrust two half-crowns at the driver, picked up his holdall and ran up the steps into the entrance hall. While the lift took him up to the fourth floor he looked at himself in the mirrored sides. Yes, not bad at all, despite the train journey. Compactly built and of average height, he looked trim and neat in his blue greatcoat. He needed a shave, but the light stubble which matched his thin brown hair hardly showed. The usually grave blue eyes, slitted by years of concentrated peering through binoculars, gleamed back at him in a gay reflection of his mood. Not the sort of man to stand out in a crowd, he concluded, but good enough to have charmed the glamorous Sonia into the 'love, honour and obey' business. He remembered his smug satisfaction the morning after the wedding, when the *Daily Bulletin* had printed a picture of the wedding and a caption which had described Sonia as *the most beautiful ballerina in London.*

The lift stopped and the self-closing doors shut behind him as he walked softly across the corridor to Flat 401. The Yale key slid in with a slight, almost imperceptible rasp and turned easily. He hung his coat and hat in the tiny hall and shut the door carefully. He noticed, without thinking, that Sonia had acquired a new camel-hair coat.

Then he crossed the drawing room, with its dining alcove, and paused outside the bedroom door. A grin of anticipation twisted his lips and he threw open the door.

She lay as he had imagined, but not asleep; neither was the man lying beside her. She stared at him with eyes that were neither blue, nor violet, nor any other colour. They seemed to have gone opaque with fright. Her mouth opened and closed very slightly, as though she was trying to say something but could not form the words.

Masefield stood rigid and ridiculously to attention, his power to think or move paralysed by the shock. His eyes remained fixed on Sonia, who lay beneath a thin sheet with her body clearly etched in its folds until the long legs vanished in the confusion of eiderdown and blankets at the foot of the four-poster. His mind took in the disorder of the room, the clothes thrown about as though hastily discarded and the jacket of a man's suit only half concealed under a crumpled cocktail dress. 'I shall only wear this dress when I'm with you, darling. You're the only person who should see what it shows.' He had been happily proud when she wore it the first time and made that silly promise.

He knew without really looking that the man had black curly hair, and, in an odd, detached sort of way, he felt disgust at the stain of greasy hair oil on what had been his pillow. He had never used hair oil, just water, and the stain could have been caused only by many nights of contact with that dirty head. The man gazed up at the four-poster's canopy with fierce intensity, an extra in the silent drama taking place between husband and wife — an old-fashioned drama, yet fiercely new now.

Thank God he's a stranger, thought Masefield with sudden clarity. *Drive me bloody mad if he was someone I knew. Poor bastard's probably as frightened by this as I am.*

The late nights, parties and petulant complaints in Sonia's letters came to life with a real meaning as he wilted against the door, struggling to control the sickness welling in his stomach. His cheeks were flaming; his ears hummed with the vibration of taut nerves. He was about to murmur something facetious — one should be facetious in this sort of situation, he thought stupidly — when his eyes moved almost automatically to the floor near his feet and a fresh wave of fury rose inside him. Sonia's pillows, lying end to end.

'Sorry about that four-poster, Sonia.' His words slapped her savagely. 'Still, you are the trying type and you never know when a man might refuse to use the floor and take you in bed. Tragic scene, this, you know. Almost like one of your modern ballets, isn't it?'

As he left the flat, he heard the owner of the camel-hair coat announce clearly, 'Sonia, you're a bitch. You never told me you were married.'

The binoculars dropped from his eyes and he looked at Boland steadily, forcing back the misery that betrayed him. 'My personal affairs are none of your business, Pilot.'

Boland looked at him shrewdly. 'All right, John. If that's the way you feel. But you never stopped talking about her before, so the change is a bit sudden, you know.' As he finished speaking he realized he had goaded Masefield too far.

'Boland, I'll tell you once more. Shut up and mind your own business. If you did that a bit more often, you might not be such a bloody washout as a navigator. You're a useless article for anyone to carry around in this war.'

Boland stared straight ahead, his face expressionless but his mind racing with excitement. He hardly heard Masefield murmur an apology for losing his temper. Instead, he thought that at the next opportunity he would go to London. It would be easy to run into Sonia — accidentally, of course.

'Echo bearing 330 degrees, sir.'

The asdic operator's report cracked through the private thoughts of the two officers. Masefield tracked the echo with the operator, immediately recognizing it as a possible submarine.

'Sound action stations, Pilot.'

Boland's fingers pressed hard on the brass button and the clanging alarm bells racketed round the ship.

2

'What does it sound like, Number One?'

'Pretty certain sub contact, sir. But hard to tell in these waters. Bearing 332 and moving slowly right.'

'Signalman, hoist investigative flag. Slow ahead both engines. Coxswain, steer 340 degrees.'

'Aye, aye, sir.'

Strong was in command of his ship. 'Stand by depth charges. Range and bearing, Number One?'

'Bearing 335, sir. Range 1000 yards.'

'Coxswain, steer 345 degrees. Yeoman, down investigative and hoist attacking flag.'

'Aye, aye, sir.'

A speck of light blinked from ahead of the convoy. '*Firefly* calling, sir,' cried the Yeoman. 'Message says: "Keep him down at least until after dark."'

At that moment Boland fixed their position on the chart and set the attack plot. Suddenly he jerked forward over the chart and, in consternation, called out, 'Captain, sir. We can't attack here. We're right in the middle of the mine barrier.'

Strong leapt into the chartroom, glanced at the Navigator's position tracks on the chart and jumped back to the bridge. 'Range and bearing, Number One?'

'Bearing 338, range 800 yards, sir.'

The Captain stared out ahead, tension pulling tightly at his face muscles. If he dropped depth charges on top of the mines, he would blow up the ship and probably set off a chain reaction that would explode every mine in the field. Yet if that submarine…

Impossible. No submarine could have penetrated this far into the field and survived. The asdic must be pinging on a shoal of fish, perhaps a wreck.

'Bearing 340, range 700, sir.'

This was something the leader had not foreseen during the working-up exercises. No procedure was laid down for dealing with this sort of problem — but then, commanding officers were supposed to use their own initiative in unexpected crises. Strong gave his orders decisively.

'Down attacking flag, Yeoman. Send to *Firefly*: "Have abandoned hunt owing to presence of mines. Contact uncertain and do not consider submarine would have penetrated minefield to this extent."'

While the signal was being sent, it was almost possible to hear the relief sighing across the bridge. The lower-deck personnel thought it more than likely that had the contact been certain, the Old Man might well have attacked and risked blowing up his ship.

'*Firefly* calling, sir,' reported the Yeoman. '"To *Concord*: What minefield? We passed deep-mine barrier ten miles to port. Carry out search procedure."'

For a moment Strong was silent. Then he regained control of himself and his ship. 'Hard-a-starboard. Full ahead both engines … one hundred and twenty revolutions. Coxswain, midships, steer 355 degrees. Number One, we will box the area and carry out search procedure. Mister Boland, check your charts for any alteration of the minefield positions.'

Not too long before the war Boland's editor had said, 'Peter, go to the royal premiere tonight and lead off your column with some sort of attack on the palace advisers for allowing the royal family to hobnob with the German ambassador. There's going to be a war, you know, despite his Lordship's editorials.'

Boland had groaned at this assignment, and early that evening had drunk too many cocktails at a film party. The next morning he awoke in a strange flat in bed with a well-known actress. He had forgotten the premiere and missed an extraordinary demonstration against the German ambassador. It had nearly ruined his career.

Now the same sick sensation gripped his stomach: self-disgust mingled with the certain knowledge that no hurried excuses could undo the damage. His wits numbed and his suave tongue silenced, he thumbed automatically through the recent 'Notices to Mariners'. As he did so, his own guilt was gradually transferred in his mind to Midshipman Harry Prentice. It was his fault, of course.

After lunch yesterday he had sent Prentice to the chartroom to make the necessary corrections to the charts that. they might need on this trip. He had other plans for spending the afternoon — plans that included a flattering letter to Joan Filbury in which, ironically, he had over-emphasized his own importance to the ship, and the writing of an unsigned article for the *Daily Bulletin.* The article concerned the type of officers being selected to command the 'little ships' in the war's most important battle. Neither the letter nor the article had been censored by another officer according to regulations, but that sort of thing rarely worried Boland. He had taken the letters to the wardroom, borrowed the censor stamp and dispatched them with the last post ashore.

Thoughts of Joan Filbury made him wince. Strong would keel-haul him for this, and Joan was in a position, as Captain D's secretary, to see all confidential reports. His chances with her would fall to zero, and he began to wonder seriously how this blunder could be blamed on Prentice. No, that would be not only impossible but bad tactics. He was the Navigator, and the Navy did not take kindly to passing the buck in such circumstances. Strong would confine the responsibility to him alone — as he had done yesterday.

Boland's lips compressed angrily as he recalled with bitter self-pity the events of their last day in harbour…

'This ship is a bitch — a ruddy, floating, inconsistent, unfaithful and undependable bitch. She's fit for the scrapheap and there's bugs in the seams, cockroaches in the cabins and rats everywhere. But like lunatics in a loony bin we seem to get along. Here we are, gentlemen, the wardroom.'

A tall, dark lieutenant, wearing the wavy stripes of the Royal Naval Volunteer Reserve, escorted two others into the wardroom of HMS *Concord*. Lieutenant Peter Boland was handsome in this particular uniform and knew it. For that reason, he had no intention of permitting the more rugged side of war to mar his perfection.

A journalist by profession and a persistent chaser of women, money and power, he had become the favourite columnist of the press baron who owned the *Daily Bulletin*. On September 2, 1939, the *Bulletin* had appeared with an editorial condemning the government for pursuing a policy destined to take the country to war. When, the very next day, the Prime Minister had made his declaration, the baron had been undismayed. The telephone switchboard which handled calls from as many correspondents as the Foreign Office had ambassadors, and from as many places, soon traced the First Sea Lord. And a few minutes later the baron committed the *Bulletin* to war by receiving a promise that if he applied through proper channels

Peter Boland would in due course become an officer in His Majesty's Navy.

When Boland answered the summons to the baron's office, he was pounced upon by a tailor who began fussing around him while one of the most powerful newspaper proprietors in Fleet Street gave his instructions. 'Tomorrow's front page will show the *Bulletin* to be in the van of self-sacrifice, m'boy. *You* —' Boland still recoiled when he remembered the emphasis in his master's voice — '*you* will be the first journalist to answer the call to duty. I've already arranged a commission in the Navy, and we'll have a picture of you in a mock-up uniform with a suitable story. Write it yourself.'

There could be no protest, no appeal. Peter Boland was in the Navy, but since that day he had never left the service of the *Daily Bulletin.* Regulations forbade officers and men to write for the press without permission. And if the Admiralty suspected that the occasional articles about the war at sea which appeared in the *Bulletin* under a neutral name came from Peter Boland, they gave no sign of it. Certainly, the articles themselves could give no cause for complaint.

During one leave in London, the baron had told him, 'When this is all over, m'boy, it's politics for you, with m'backing. You need a rich wife, preferably American, but a poor English one will do if she's got a title.' After that it had not been in Boland to resist the temptation to imagine himself a future cabinet minister.

Now he introduced the new officers joining *Concord* to Midshipman Harry Prentice, RNR, sole occupant of the wardroom at that time of day, and ordered pink gins all round.

'You will notice,' he continued, 'that she has four funnels, in itself a curious phenomenon. This, m'dear fellows —' he studiously copied the press baron's abbreviation of 'my' — 'is because you have the dubious honour and privilege to join one of fifty such oddities so generously presented to us by our glorious American allies. Remember the Bermuda deal? Now you know the meaning of selling one's soul for a pittance. No doubt of it, m'dear chaps, Uncle Sam had his tongue stuck firmly in his cheek over that deal. This goddamn veteran of — well, it can't be more recent than the civil war — can buck your belly out in a flat calm, pitch and toss when at anchor, and roll your eyeballs out in dry dock. Our motto here is, never take the bloody thing to sea unless we have to. If we can't help doing that, then we try to confine our warlike activities to the summer months; and if that's not possible, then we make every effort to avoid really rough weather. Take m'word for it, if we should ever hit any she will turn over like a barbecued roast on a spit, and neither you, nor I, nor the rats will survive.'

He emptied his glass with a flourish while the 'dear fellows' gazed at him a little blankly, uncertain whether to laugh or take this strange officer seriously. Lieutenant Kenneth Grant, RNVR, had six weeks' training and even less practical sea experience behind him; Sub-Lieutenant Christopher Sterling had arrived straight from King Alfred training school. Appointments to *Concord* had been the beginning of war for both of them, an exciting prelude to the vast canvas of fire and battle each believed would be his lot in the future. Neither could foresee that no human enemy had yet equalled the weather in ferocity or single-mindedness.

Grant, a City of London bank clerk from a suburban home, looked around the wardroom with a sense of satisfaction. At the far end was the table already set for about ten officers; facing it on one side was the serving hatch to the officers' pantry. A few feet from him the Midshipman sat huddled behind a newspaper in a deep leather club armchair, one of three in the anteroom. Down the ship's side was a wide leather settee. Round three sides was a framed and enlarged series of the famous 'Jane' strip cartoon, presented to the wardroom by the *Daily Mirror*.

An electric fire burned in the grate of an old-fashioned fuel-burning stove. This would really be something for him to talk about when he next visited the Northwood Sports Club, something to impress the girls. Although stocky, Grant was well proportioned, dark and square-faced. He looked quizzically at Peter Boland, his brown eyes showing interest. He was thinking, *There's a man with a Savile Row tailor and a hand-to-mouth bank account — a man I'd have to check on before cashing his cheque for a quid.*

His branch manager would have been pleased at this snap judgment. Boland's account was indeed a permanently perilous venture, which would not have been tolerated had it not been for the known relationship between himself and his owner.

Chris Sterling was a slender, fair boy, not yet twenty-one, and unlikely to receive the key of the front door when he did reach adulthood. His father was a North Country businessman with a proven flair for making the 'brass'. Chris had not shown any signs of inheriting this flair; his sole achievement to date had been to cultivate the North Country out of his accent.

He was more uncertain of his new surroundings than Grant, more awed by Boland's obvious sophistication and general air of cynical boredom. Both knew they were being shown round by a writer with a brilliant future; Boland had told them so himself.

The nineteen-year-old Midshipman looked up from the morning paper and interrupted Boland's flow of rhetoric. 'Damn it, Boland, must you talk so much bilge? These chaps might believe it.'

The fact that the new officers were his seniors was not one that would easily deter Harry Prentice. He spoke from the safe heights of an old hand in familiar country and, in his brief career so far, no one had challenged him at the first meeting. *After all,* he would often think, *I am a professional sailor compared with these blasted civilian pansies with stripes on.* Brash in most things, he felt inferior only in one: he was not a gentleman, and the attainment of this distinction had become his most serious, if dubious, ambition.

In discussing his Merchant Navy days, he made a point of depreciating his former colleagues and superiors, even blatantly dismissing them as uncouth, which they were not. His understanding of the term 'gentleman' was immature and superficial and not in the least concerned with character. He considered Boland a gentleman, and was surprised at the obvious amusement this caused in the wardroom, Boland included.

Only the Captain and First Lieutenant frightened him; he quaked a little in their presence and took great care to always address them with a respectful 'sir'. Still very young, he was fearful of any real authority.

But he was jealous of his few years at sea as an apprentice, and regarded himself as infinitely superior to Boland as a navigator. His resentment at having to assist the Navigator came out in odd pockets of resistance; for instance, when sent to the chartroom to correct charts he would dawdle and do slipshod work, for which the Captain was continually blaming Boland. But being lazy himself, Boland did nothing to discipline the Mid, and their spasmodic forays into the irksome duties of the Navigator's department rarely accomplished their object. Now Boland turned on him.

'I shall not tell you again, Mid. As far as you are concerned, my name is never just Boland. It is Pilot, perhaps Peter, and even an occasional 'sir' would not be objectionable. But not Boland.'

Prentice flushed, and sought shelter behind his newspaper as the Navigator turned again to the new arrivals.

'It's not only the ship that's out of place in this Navy; oh, no. Our Mid is also an oddity, quite an offensive one, at that. To please him, you have to learn little ditties like *"Eight bells and the watch is o'er; Here comes the lousy twelve to four."* He's like that. Comes from being an apprentice in tramps.'

Prentice, now thoroughly mortified, searched for an answer to the sting in Boland's words, but his limited vocabulary could muster only a two-word phrase which he knew instinctively to be vulgar and therefore inadequate. He was saved from further embarrassment by the bosun's mate knocking on the wardroom door and reporting to Boland, 'Officer of the Day, sir. Captain's coming.'

The Navigator picked up his cap from the table and hurried out to the midships gangway, arriving just in time to receive aboard Lieutenant-Commander Louis Strong, RNR, commanding officer of *Concord.* Strong returned the salute and muttered quickly, 'Come along to my cabin, Pilot. I want a word with you.'

Boland followed, frowning. It could be sailing orders or it might concern something he had forgotten to do. An invitation to the Captain's cabin at this time of day could mean only more work or trouble.

The Captain pushed aside the door curtain to his cabin, threw down a briefcase and settled himself in the large swivel chair at his desk. Boland stood to attention with his cap hugged tightly under his left arm. Strong looked at him thoughtfully for a second and then began speaking in a quiet, unhurried voice in which anger was only thinly veiled.

'Mister Boland —' he invariably reverted to the Merchant Service 'mister' when irritated — 'are our charts corrected up to date?'

So that's it, thought Boland. *He's been poking about the chartroom.*

'No, sir.'

'Why not?'

'I'm afraid there's not been much time, sir. You see —'

Strong's gesture of annoyance interrupted the explanation.

'No time, Mister Boland? And you have the Midshipman as an assistant?' His eyes mocked the Navigator. 'I'll tell you why: because both the Mid and you are idle and like going ashore too much. Yesterday you visited a friend in *Stork* in the forenoon and stayed away all day. The day before that you found an excuse to call at Captain D's office, where you played lovey-dovey with his Wren secretary. You left no instructions for the Mid, so he mooned about the wardroom all day trying to drink as much as you. I talked to Captain D's secretary this morning, Mister Boland, and she tells me you are taking her to a cinema this afternoon. For her sake, this ship can sail into uncharted minefields, wrecks, rocks and what have you — is that so, Mister Boland?'

Winchester College, Oxford and eight years of journalism had provided Boland with a thick, protective skin. But he was not insensitive, and now a fury welled up inside him that Strong should have discovered his affair with Joan Filbury. Silly bitch! Why couldn't she keep her mouth shut?

'You are going to change your ways, whether you like it or not,' Strong continued mercilessly. 'I have taken the liberty of informing Miss Filbury that you will be unable to meet her this afternoon. She quite understood, Mister Boland. She mentioned that of all the officers in this port who take her out you seem to have the most free time.' He smiled to himself at the clear evidence on the Navigator's face that the thrust had reached home. No longer expressionless, it was almost redly indignant. 'You will bring those charts up to date this afternoon instead,' Strong finished abruptly. 'And make the Mid work with you. Is that clear?'

'Yes, quite.'

Damn fool, thought Strong, to think that the deliberate omission of the 'sir' would provoke him. 'One more thing, Mister Boland. Since the First Lieutenant abandoned his leave and returned to the ship, he has been carrying out duties which you other officers should have taken over while we were short-handed. But you have made not the slightest effort to help him. Now the two new officers have brought the wardroom up to strength, I expect you to start pulling your weight and help Number One to break them in. Any more slacking and I'll have you transferred to big ships. You wouldn't like that, would you?'

Boland was silent, and Strong felt a sudden distaste for the man who had forced the unpleasant scene upon him. 'That's all.'

'Aye, aye, sir.'

Boland left the cabin with a straight back reflecting his outraged dignity. After all, he was a friend of peers and destined for a great political future. It seemed to him that Strong didn't quite understand who he was and the extent of his influence.

He was wrong. Strong knew exactly who he was and, for that reason, the grim smile which followed Boland's departure held more than a hint of sadness.

Louis Strong was French-Canadian, born and raised in the 'Little Montparnasse' of Montreal. He had joined the Canadian Pacific Steamship Company twenty years ago as an apprentice, and when war broke out he was First Mate of a passenger liner.

Now, at thirty-six, he was commanding officer of a destroyer. His reputation was solid, although he neither knew nor cared about it. Each 'flimsy' written by previous commanding officers recorded the vital facts — that he was efficient, reliable, and took the war and his duties seriously. The last of the reports had come from the most famous of all Liverpool leaders, Captain Johnnie Walker, and it had been this one that had recommended him for a command of his own.

Concord was no passenger liner, nor was she a thing of beauty, but she was his ship, and Louis Strong was determined that the faith in him expressed by such captains as Walker should not be trifled with by such as Boland.

Strong was an average man; average in height and looks. His square, rugged face under the slightly greying black hair was neither handsome nor particularly ugly. He did not think of himself as an intellectual, or even clever; neither did he class himself as a moron. If he had been asked about his ambitions, his most probable reply would have been, 'I shall be content if life demands nothing more of me than to be a sailor, and a good one.'

Yet life was already demanding more; it had expected him to volunteer to fight a war, and now dictated that he should command a valuable warship with a crew of 150 officers and men who relied upon him to bring them safely through the natural hazards of the sea and the almost daily attacks of the enemy.

This was taxing his ability to the limit, for again it was an average ability, that was no more and no less than was expected of him. He recognized failings in his personal character and was unable to master them; he suffered from a violent inferiority complex when in the presence of very senior officers. He resented the occasional reminders, more often than not made jokingly, that he was a colonial. The word implied narrow provinciality and therefore should not be used, in his opinion, unless in terms of insult. Sometimes his efforts to evade the issue of his background — and he cursed himself for being a weak fool when this mood came upon him — rebounded viciously and gave him the very characteristics he despised.

Only at sea was he truly at home. Officers of all nations, creeds and backgrounds fought together, and he felt that no one gave a damn if his shipmate was commercial traveller, chimney-sweep or nobleman, just so long as he was efficient. It was only those seemingly uncomplicated, smug bastards ashore who got him down.

In this he was wrong, dreadfully wrong.

He could not understand that those same bastards had, in fact, recognized in him the qualities for which he had been given a command — unshakable integrity, obvious coolness in action and an unerring instinct for assessing emergencies quickly and accurately. Therefore they joked and pulled his leg at moments when he wanted to be serious, because it is the Englishman's way to be casual with those who are his equals and never to allow them to see his affection or respect. That this would be an intolerable show of emotion for an Englishman escaped the Latin-bred Strong, and he continued to dislike those who admired him most.

He settled deeper into his chair and concentrated on the voyage ahead. *Concord* belonged to the 5th Escort Group, a highly trained and seasoned team of six ships — two destroyers and four corvettes — and 500 men. They would meet Convoy ON 98 in the North Channel, off the coast of Northern Ireland, tomorrow evening. Six ships to shepherd forty merchantmen across 2000 miles of Atlantic, and through whatever U-boat wolfpacks might lie waiting in their path. How many, he wondered, would reach St John's safely? Last trip they had lost twelve; it had been seventeen the trip before.

His mind switched to his officers. John Masefield, the First Lieutenant, was invaluable. Good-humoured, even-tempered and a deliberate thinker even at the worst moments, he was popular with the crew and took no nonsense from anyone. More important, the crew respected him. But he wished Number One would not seem so supercilious when his Captain forgot formal naval procedure. Then Strong's sense of fairness chided him for allowing his infernal inferiority complex to rear up again. Of course Masefield was never supercilious, he was incapable of it.

Why had Masefield abandoned his leave so abruptly? His excuse that Sonia was away did not hold water. Transparently that was what it was, just an excuse. Good God, he hoped there was nothing wrong with that marriage. Surely not; it had always seemed happy enough. Whatever happened, Masefield must not be allowed to work off steam to the extent of cracking up. Blast these women. Had they no sense? Didn't they see how important they were to the fighting efficiency of the men at war? No, of course not. Half the leave-breaking in Liverpool was caused by women, mostly wives and sweethearts.

For the past week Number One had been working like mad getting the ship ready for sea again. These two new officers would take a load off his shoulders, something Boland should have done days ago. The thought struck him suddenly that if anything happened to Masefield, Boland would have to take over as First Lieutenant. Somehow the idea didn't appal him nearly as much as it might have done. In any case, he would have to talk to Masefield about Boland, the Mid, and his personal affairs at home.

His face softened as he thought of the Engineer Officer, Lieutenant (E) Ian Murray, a dour but able Scot, so typical of his race, so bloody efficient and un-excitable. Yes, he was lucky to have the always-willing help of Number One and the Chief. If the ship was a warlike unit at all, it was mainly due to these two.

What about the new chaps, Grant and Sterling? Grant seemed all right and, by all accounts, had made some effort to learn during his very brief sojourn in his last ship. Sterling was different. Obviously a highly sensitive boy — he probably suffered from too much mothering as a child — he was too timid, too shy. Strong had met them both ashore at Derby House that morning, and Sterling had been stammering with fear. *Well,* he supposed, *we can't all be free of Freudian knots.* The boy would probably get over it, but he would have to be watched closely. There might well be just the ingredients of panic there.

He got up from the chair and walked to the washbasin to rinse his hands. A few minutes later he was approaching the wardroom when Masefield's voice, low-pitched and angry, made him pause.

'For God's sake, Pilot, stop talking about your sordid love affairs. To be honest, I'm bloody glad the Old Man torpedoed your date this afternoon. It's about time you did some work around here.'

Strong grinned and strode diffidently into the wardroom. As the officers stood to greet him, he said lightly, 'Well, well. It really looks as though I shall have the pleasure of lunching with all my officers today. Nice change. Glad to see everyone hard at it.'

He turned to a steward to order a drink, and only Boland and Masefield caught the irony in his voice. Number One chuckled derisively at the Navigator: he knew now what the rest of Boland's interview with the Captain had been about.

Strong looked at Grant and Sterling. 'Have you been round the ship yet?'

'Yes, sir.' Grant answered for both. 'Lieutenant Boland and the Midshipman have taken us around.'

'Any questions?'

'No, not yet, sir —'

But Sterling intervened. 'Yes, please, sir.' His voice faltered and his face was pale with embarrassment as the wardroom went silent.

'What is it, Sub?'

'It's about something Lieutenant Boland was saying earlier, sir. He says these destroyers are death traps in rough weather. Is that true, sir?'

Strong resisted the temptation to laugh, feeling that this was a serious moment for the young officer. 'Of course not, Sub. Anything can happen in storms, but this ship is as good as any other. Take a lot to sink her. Why?'

Sterling hesitated and then gazed earnestly at Strong. 'Well, sir, I never really wanted to go to sea — join the Navy, I mean — because I hate storms. Once I went sailing in a dinghy on the Solent and we capsized in a squall. I panicked a bit, sir, and swore I'd never sail again. I hated it.'

Even the wardroom steward had stood still, sharing the astonishment of the officers at this candid, innocently made confession. Strong felt momentarily disgusted at such blatant baring of a soul before strangers. *Great Scott, what have I been sent this time? A babe who is already seeking a sympathetic mother among us.*

Curiously, it was Boland who broke the silence. 'Not to worry, Sub. Only leg-pulling, that's all.'

Strong looked at him in surprise and said in a pleasant, reassuring voice, 'It must have been a nasty experience, Sterling. But we've all had some such lucky escape in our time, you know. And, as Pilot says, you must not take him too seriously. Most of us just ignore him. Now, Number One, how about lunch?'

As they took their places at the table, the Midshipman's eyes were fixed on Boland, shining with malicious joy. Revenge was none the less sweet for being exacted by the Captain.

Boland turned another page of the Notices. There it was: Notice to Mariners, Number 1012. *The deep-mine barrier laid in the North Channel in accordance with Admiralty Fleet Order 10/206/2/12 is amended in accordance with Commander-in-Chief, Western Approaches signal of November 20/42.*

My God, how could that young fool have missed anything as plain as that? Of all the inefficient clots!

His anger died quickly and a faint smile crossed his face as he thought of the pot calling the kettle names. Boland was not particularly fair-minded when his own hide was at stake, but his sense of humour sometimes compensated for this; he was too intelligent not to recognize some of his faults.

While Strong and Masefield continued the search for the suspected submarine, Boland fixed the ship's position and amended the mined area on the charts. He looked ruefully at the result: *Firefly* had been only too right. They were well clear of mines, and if the contact had been a U-boat, then it survived because of him. For once he was not proud of his achievement and, for the first time, approached the threshold of humility.

He looked hard at Strong's bent back. 'Captain, sir.'

'Yes, what is it?'

'*Firefly* was correct. We are well clear of the minefield. Charts are corrected and our position amended, sir.'

'Thank you, Mister Boland.' Strong's voice was normal, not even raised. Boland returned to the chartroom, puzzled that the expected outburst had not been forthcoming.

The search went on until after dusk, when Strong turned *Concord* towards the convoy, thankful that the submarine — if that was what they had been hunting — had been kept down so that it could not wireless a report of the convoy's course and speed for the night. *Concord* was surging ahead at full speed when he left the bridge with Masefield in charge as Officer of the Watch.

Boland watched him leave, convinced that the Captain had gone below to write his report of the incident — a report that Joan Filbury would be one of the first to see. Sterling arrived on the bridge to join the First Lieutenant as junior Officer of the Watch. Boland decided he might as well find out what Masefield was thinking.

'You know, Number One, that Mid is the worst kind of idiot landing me into that jam.'

'Why blame the Mid, Pilot?'

'Well, I told him to make sure the charts —'

'You're the Navigator, not the Mid,' Masefield interrupted.

'I suppose you're going to hold this against me as well,' Boland muttered petulantly.

Masefield was almost sorry for him. 'No, that's not my job. It's the Captain's. I just happen to believe that once again you're your own worst enemy.'

'Oh, for Christ's sake, don't start moralizing now, Number One.'

'I'm not,' replied Masefield with the first signs of exasperation. 'But even if I was, why not? You've been heading for some sort of mess like this for weeks, and in my opinion — since you have virtually asked for it — you deserve whatever the Old Man hands out.'

Boland glared back at the First Lieutenant until the steady, grave blue eyes forced him to turn away and leave the bridge.

'Looks like we're heading into some dirty weather, sir.'

Kenneth Grant handed the signal pad to Strong as he came up to the bridge. The top message was an Admiralty signal giving warning of gales south of Greenland. The Captain's brow creased thoughtfully.

'You may be right, Grant. Glass is going down pretty steadily too. Still, we've had it fine for the last ten days.'

It was 1000 on December 12, and already rumours had spread through the ships of the convoy: St John's for Christmas.

Strong was beginning to like Grant. He had learned quickly and had been given charge of the forenoon and first watch at night with Warrant Officer Tom Bellows, known to the ship as 'Guns', as his junior. Like Boland, Grant was reliable enough for Strong to be sure that when in doubt he would obey standing orders to call the Captain. That was in Boland's favour anyway, he thought grimly.

'Incidentally, how's Doc this morning?'

'Doesn't look good, sir. He suffers a lot from these bouts of malaria. And I think he feels seasick most of the time as well.'

'Hmm.' Strong looked round the horizon. 'Hope this weather holds off for a bit. I'll be in my cabin for a while, Grant. You might tell the First Lieutenant I'd like to see him.'

'Aye, aye, sir.'

Five minutes later, Masefield reported to the Captain, who was lying on his bunk fully dressed, obviously worried.

'Number One, I'm wondering about Leading Seaman Minns. If there is anything wrong with him we ought to be told soon.'

'Doc thinks it might be a grumbling appendix, sir.'

'How is Doc?'

'Malaria coming on again.'

'Good God, what a time! Tell him he has until tomorrow morning to decide if Minns needs an operation and whether he will be fit enough to perform it himself. If not, we can have Minns transferred to *Firefly* or one of the merchant ships which might be carrying a doctor. I can't leave it any later than that because the weather is rising.'

'Yes, sir. I'll go and see him now.'

'And Number One —'

'Yes, sir?'

'Have lifelines ready for rigging along the upper deck. I have a feeling we are in for a rough passage.'

3

The night of December 12, 1942, was the night of the moon and the wind. For a hundred miles in any direction from Convoy ON 98, ships sailed under a curiously bright moon that shone with bleak intensity behind dark feathery clouds racing up from the west to absorb the moonbeams in a pale watery mist. It was the coming of the storm.

The swell had shortened to rough corrugations which rapped resoundingly against *Concord*'s stem. As midnight approached, the signal pad grew thick with warnings of cyclones, depressions and hurricanes, an ominous timetable of danger. Barometers fell, steadied, then fell again, and convoys wide apart and sailing in opposite directions approached the storm area stripped for action against the natural and traditional enemy — the sea.

They sailed without alteration of course, their routes established by implacable authority and their crews recognizing that the U-boat was but a puny obstruction compared with the gathering power of wind and sea.

Strong lay on his bunk, wearing uniform and sea boots, snatching this brief respite before the full force of the weather hit the convoy. He had no illusions about the hardships the days ahead would bring, or of the grim struggle he would have to keep *Concord* afloat. It would be a severe test, not only of his skill, but of her stability and the integrity of her builders.

The bosun's mate stood in the open doorway. 'Ten minutes to eight bells, sir.'

'Very good, Bosun's Mate.'

Strong fought himself upright and stood for a moment wearily wrapping himself in the coats and mufflers needed to keep out the worst of the cold. Outside, he bent against the wind and clambered up the ladder to the bridge. Grant and Guns greeted him in the darkness while he stood with his eyes tightly shut until they could forget the red blackout lights below and become accustomed to the pale moonglow.

'Weather getting up a bit, eh?' he called out, stating the obvious more for the sake of putting the two junior officers at their ease than for any other reason.

'Yes, sir, it is. Pretty ominous, too. Rather like a brilliant glow outside Dante's Inferno.'

Strong grimaced to himself at this evidence of a poetic mind. 'You'll get used to this sort of thing, Grant. Weather usually behaves a bit strangely before a storm.' He paused. 'And I agree, it does make an attractive scene tonight, in a frightening sort of way.'

'Does that mean it will be bad, sir?' asked Grant quietly.

'Good heavens, all storms are bad. No, not particularly so, I shouldn't think.'

'We've had the lifelines rigged, just in case, sir,' Guns intervened.

'Thanks, Guns. Isn't it time for the change of watch?' There was considerable scuffling and muttering going on around the bridge in the darkness as the middle watch arrived to take over — lookouts, quartermaster, bosun's mate, asdic operator and messenger.

'Yes, just about, sir,' replied Grant anxiously. 'But Lieutenant Boland and the Mid are always a couple of minutes late.'

Strong realized that Grant was not intentionally sneaking, but he wished the man had had the sense not to say that sort of thing. The punctual arrival of reliefs was a fetish, and it was

Number One's job to see that officers set a good example to the men. How could an officer take action against a rating for being late if he was himself guilty of the same offence? Now that it had come up, he would have to talk to Number One about it in the morning.

His mind could not dwell on the point for long. Surgeon-Lieutenant Tim Goodwin had contracted another bout of malaria, Leading Seaman Minns had developed acute appendicitis, and the weather was such that by morning there would be little hope of transferring Minns or having a doctor sent aboard.

Yet these problems, nicely in the balance, must be subordinated to his primary concern of protecting the rear of the convoy. His eyes gleamed with a quick flash of humour — malaria in an Atlantic winter, what a ruddy paradox!

Louis Strong's worries could ease or become worse. They became worse the next morning with the arrival of an Admiralty signal addressed to the 5th Escort Group and the Commodore.

'There are indications of eight U-boats in your vicinity,' read the signal. And shortly before dawn *Firefly* confirmed the enemy's presence by reporting HF/DF bearings on a chattering U-boat some twenty miles away. Visibility had closed down to little more than four miles, hiding all but the rear ships of the columns in a dull black mist.

Concord's bows were beginning to plunge deeply into every wave, sending gushers of spray over the bridge. At 7.30 a.m. Masefield, in charge of the morning watch, called down the voice-pipe to the Captain's cabin, 'It's seven-thirty, sir.' He listened for signs that Strong was coming awake, replied to a query about the weather with a fervent 'Bloody,' and continued, '*Vine*'s dropped back to pass on a signal from *Firefly,* sir. Signalman is reading it now.'

'Right, Number One, I'm coming up.'

A few minutes later Strong stumbled up to the bridge and sat heavily on his wooden seat behind the gyro compass. The signalman handed him a pad showing the signal relayed on by the corvette *Vine*:

'To *Concord*: From *Firefly* — In view presence of large enemy concentration in our vicinity cannot approve you leaving station for transfer of patient which in any event might prove impossible in present weather. If your doctor unfit to supervise operation mine will give instructions over R/T.'

'Good God!' The exclamation came from Strong involuntarily.

Matthews, the sick-bay attendant, lit a cigarette for the stocky West Country man lying painfully in the sick-bay bunk. He had been a nurse at Guy's Hospital in London before conscription had snatched him up and deposited him at the Royal Naval Barracks, Devonport. Once there, he had been subjected to the traditional raucous barrage: 'What, a ruddy nurse with pants on? Blimey, matey, you waits till the Navy gets 'old of yer proper. Know anything about medicine, chum? Then the Navy'll make yer a ruddy stoker.'

But the Navy had proved very conscious indeed of his qualifications. A few weeks of drilling and training in Naval medical formalities had ended with his drafting to *Concord.*

Minns' appendix was going to get out of hand soon, and Doc was in no shape to do much about it. Could he do it himself? No, he would not like responsibility for that operation even if Doc could shout instructions from his bed. 'You're going to be OK, Micky,' he said quietly to the dark-faced

Minns. 'The Old Man's getting *Firefly*'s doc over to take the ruddy thing out.'

Matthews had been a good nurse and he wanted to do his best for his mates aboard *Concord*. Although neither a deep thinker nor especially sensitive, he instinctively realized that the men wanted to trust him in the event of illness or battle wounds, so he reacted by working hard to earn that trust. In doing so, he had also acquired the confidence of Doc.

Tim Goodwin lay in the bunk against the bulkhead opposite to Minns in the sick bay, which was also his cabin. A tall, spare and gingery-haired man of twenty-seven, he had once been assistant to Graves, the finest brain surgeon in London. When the German hordes overran Europe he had been pondering upon his future while walking in St James's Park until his gaunt, bony face had looked up to find he was outside Queen Anne's, headquarters of the Admiral Commanding Reserves. Obviously, he had thought later, his feet had known the answer before his brain. 'And me a brain man, too', he would say when repeating the story.

A doorman had asked what he wanted and his wide mouth had slipped into a shy, crooked grin as he asked if the Navy could use a surgeon. During the subsequent interview with a senior Surgeon-Captain, he had apologized for specializing and was astonished that somehow this did not affect his acceptance. He would have been even more surprised had he been told that Graves had later informed the Admiralty privately that Tim Goodwin was one of his most promising young assistants.

After a refresher course in general medicine, Goodwin had been sent to Singapore, but his stay had been short. In February of that year he had retreated with the rest from the

Japanese flood and at the same time contracted malaria fever. Ever since, no matter where he was, the bouts would recur — sometimes intense, often slight, but always certain to come.

Now he slept in his bunk fitfully while Matthews comforted the stricken and understandably scared Minns. Appendicitis at sea was the subject of mess-deck jokes and associated with galley carving knives and amateurs. But, like car accidents or getting run over, it was something that never happened except to other people. Minns knew, without reasoning, that it was happening to him.

All bottles and instruments had been locked away in compartments to prevent breakages in the rising sea. *Concord* was beginning to roll and pitch at the same time in a curious stomach-sinking corkscrew motion. Matthews steadied himself by holding on to the edge of Minns' bunk while he looked on impotently at the obvious struggle taking place to stifle the man's pain. If the operation was not carried out soon — within the next couple of hours — it would be impossible.

In the Leading Seamen's mess, Bill Gridley, the huge black-bearded gunlayer, was muttering into his mug of tea. 'What sort of bloody navy is this anyway? When you go sick you have to wait for the doc to get well first. If he ain't bein' seasick, he's sweatin' out a ruddy jungle fever. He can't cure his bleedin' self — and 'im a doc, too.'

Another leading hand, his mate in the for'ard gun's crew, laughed derisively. 'You're behind the times, Bill. Ain't you 'eard? The Old Man's asked *Firefly* to send over their doc to look after poor old Minns.'

Gridley looked up dismally. 'Docs — they're all no bloomin' good, or why they in the ruddy Navy, eh?' He blew hard on his tea, triumphantly certain that he had silenced all opposition to his pessimism.

One of the quartermasters scrambled down the ladder into the mess, threw off his oilskins and wrapped thick hands round a mug of steaming tea. 'Now, mateys,' he announced importantly, 'this is straight from the bridge.'

'About poor bloody Minns, I betcha,' murmured Gridley gloomily.

'You guessed it, Bill. *Firefly* just signalled that 'cos there's some ruddy U-boats around and the weather being what it is, they ain't gonna send over their doc and we ain't to leave station neither.' He paused to witness the effect his news had upon the mess.

'Well, get on wi' it,' demanded Gridley. 'What's the Old Man goin' to do?'

'That's just it. Nothing. *Firefly*'s doc is goin' to give instructions over the R/T.'

A murky, smoke-filled silence followed. Gridley broke it. His eyes gazed upwards at an imaginary heaven as he called out with raised hands, 'Dear Gawd, 'ave pity on poor misguided Minns. 'E ain't meant to be really sinful, just a little 'igh-spirited, sir. 'E certainly don't deserve that any of this terrible bunch of officers should make free with the knife on 'is poor defenceless body.' He looked down again with such a serious expression that the mess burst out laughing, causing him to gaze at each in turn with real amazement. 'Blimey, no wonder there's a bloody war on. It's to get rid of a few of you 'eathen, 'eartless beggars, that's what.'

After a meagre breakfast of coffee and stale, cold toast, Strong and Masefield visited the sick bay. Matthews saluted without wearing a cap and received a stern glance of disapproval from the Captain, who then bent down over Minns.

'How are you feeling?'

The sailor's reply came in gasps between attacks of pain. 'Fine, sir, thankee.'

'Well, just stick it out a little longer, Minns, and we'll have you fixed up soon.' Strong was glad to turn away to speak to Goodwin, who was now awake and propped up. His body trembled uncontrollably every few minutes.

'Doc.' Strong spoke in a low voice while Masefield and Matthews bent over Minns. 'Listen carefully. We can't transfer Minns or bring another doctor aboard. Weather and submarines. Can you operate?'

Strong was startled for a second at Goodwin's seeming lack of interest. It looked as though he might be rambling. But Goodwin controlled himself and shook his head weakly. 'No, that's impossible. Minns must have that appendix out today, this morning. Someone else will have to do it.'

'How about Matthews?'

'No.' Goodwin lifted a handkerchief to his face and wiped it clear of sweat. 'He's good at his job but it wouldn't be fair to give him that responsibility.'

Strong nodded. A mistake and Matthews would never live it down; lower-deck antagonisms died hard.

'In that case, it's impossible, Doc. No one here has ever done this sort of thing before. *Firefly*'s doctor has offered to give instructions over the R/T, but I don't see how it would help. For God's sake, can't you pull yourself together to get this done?'

This time he was sure the doctor had not heard him. Goodwin was tossing about in the bunk, throwing his head from side to side under the impact of the fever. Strong was about to leave when Goodwin's hand gripped his arm tightly. He waited for the attack to subside.

'Captain, sir, I won't be able to do it, but there will be a chance if I give the instructions from here. Then I can watch to stop anything being done wrongly. Matthews will dose me.'

'Who, Doc — who can perform this operation?'

'You, sir.'

Concord was being thrown about more than ever; the movement was not so languid, it was becoming jerky and unexpected. Strong and Masefield huddled behind the windscreens on the bridge. Only the Captain could make the decision, and Masefield was the only person from whom he would seek or take advice. For the moment, he was seeking nothing other than some way out, a way that would solve the dilemma without involving himself or Minns in a suicidal operation.

He recalled his days in small cargo boats when he had been Second Mate and the nearest approach to a doctor for thirty-odd men. His knowledge of medicine was limited to what was necessary for the administering of 'number nines' to sick sailors. But in his cabin had been a placard, carefully varnished to avoid being torn, which had given instructions on how to perform an appendicitis operation. A chart of the human body accompanied the placard, and every night for weeks he had studied it rather fearfully, quite sure that one day he would be called upon to fill a surgeon's shoes.

The day and the opportunity had passed him by, and when transferred to a bigger ship which carried not one but three doctors, he had quickly forgotten the placard. It flooded his memory now, but the instructions were blurred fragments from the past. He had given some thought to asking Masefield to operate, but somehow that placard made all the difference. It meant that he was the one with the greater qualifications.

'What do you think, Number One?'

'Well, sir, if Doc thinks he can supervise, perhaps I should try it.'

'Trying's going to be no good. There will be the one chance, and if that fails I wouldn't give tuppence for Minns.' There was a moment of silence. Then Strong sighed. 'I'll do it myself, Number One. Send down for the Chief, will you? And I want you to handle the ship until it's all over.'

Masefield sent the messenger down for the Chief and studied his captain. *What a man,* he thought. *And me, what a stupid fool. Here I am behaving as though Sonia had ruined my life, as though out of the whole world I was the only one with cares and worries. Louis Strong not only commands this ship but has a ruddy hurricane about to break on him and an operation on his hands. By God, he'll do it, too.*

Masefield's eyes brightened with confidence. Almost light-heartedly, he said, 'Can't I come down and help, sir?'

'Good God, no, John. Your job is more important than mine. All I shall do is obey Doc's orders, but you have to keep this ship from rolling about too much. One awkward movement when the knife is in and I'll probably kill Minns. You keep her head into the sea and threaten the coxswain with horrible fates if he lets the wheel get out of hand. Yeoman, which corvette is in sight?'

'I can still see *Vine,* sir.'

'Right. Ask her to pass the following to *Firefly*: "Imperative operation carried out immediately. Many thanks your offer to give medical advice over R/T but our doctor can supervise operation. Intend operating myself and request permission to alter course to minimize ship's movement."'

The Chief arrived on the bridge, his slight, small figure wrapped in overalls which whipped and cracked in the wind. He steadied himself against the wheelhouse door and reported. 'You wanted me, sir?'

'Yes, Chief. Leading Seaman Minns has to be operated on now. The sick-bay attendant is getting everything ready and the First Lieutenant will take over the bridge. What's our most comfortable speed in this weather? We'll turn into the sea, of course.'

'Anything less than 120 revolutions and she'll begin to roll a bit, sir. Say about 140.'

'I agree, Chief. Now you stay down in the engine room and see that those revolutions are maintained. Number One will let you know when it's all over.'

'Aye, aye, sir.' He turned to the ladder leading down to the cabin flat and paused. 'Best of luck, sir,' he grinned cheerfully.

Strong smiled, if only to hide the fear he felt must show in his eyes. He could never bring it off, never. Would the men ever forgive him if Minns died?

'*Vine* calling, sir.' It was the Yeoman reading the faint light from the corvette. '"*Firefly* says take any steps you consider necessary to perform successful operation. You may break R/T silence in emergency. Regret unable offer further assistance, wish you best of luck."'

'Very good, Yeoman. Number One, take over now, please. Bring her round to 295 degrees and play with the engines a bit until you think she's on best course and speed. I'm going down below for a wash. The operation will start in ten minutes.'

Ordinary Seaman (Hostilities Only) Bradley Randall leaned against a depth charge on the quarterdeck. His public-school accent piped shrilly at a sailor wedged inside the steel shelter.

Each wave brought a fresh river of water surging across the deck.

'It's true, you know, O'Flynn. My family own more than a thousand acres in Sussex. The Lord-Lieutenant of the county is my father's best friend. They hunt together, you know.'

Young Randall was not popular with his shipmates. His constant references to his family's wealth, his education and his mother's regret that he was not an officer rasped on their bored, disinterested nerves.

The Irishman leaned out to see better. 'Bejesus, ye bloody groaner, will ye stop yer yapping and keep a proper lookout. By the Holy Mary, a ruddy U-boat could sneak off our propellers and ye'd never see the rascal.'

Randall was not to be diverted. 'But, O'Flynn, it's true. And those stupid officers and that horrible little midshipman have the right to order me about. It's not fair. Why, I could buy them all out, and this ship, too. I wrote to my father and asked him to pull strings, you know.'

O'Flynn rolled his eyes and muttered exasperatedly, 'Shut yer mouth. Yer a babe that deserves to be bate, so ye do. To talk so about yer superior officers ... aw, Mother o' Gawd, what's the matter now?'

Concord had rolled hard under the helm as Masefield brought her round on to the new course. A high wave had broken amidships and swept down the quarterdeck, nearly taking Randall with it. O'Flynn jumped out of the shelter, grabbed the youngster and swung him back to safety. 'Sure we could do without ye great, me boyo, but I'd never forgive meself if I let the future owner of this ship drown before 'e'd paid the first instalment.'

The telephone buzzer rang urgently and one of the depth-charge crew lifted the receiver to his ear. It was the signalman on the bridge.

'Quarterdeck, this is Johnson 'ere. The Old Man has just gone down to operate on Minns.'

'What — you mean he's going to do it 'imself?'

''S right, chum.'

When the news had been passed round, O'Flynn stared up at the swiftly moving clouds. Even Randall could tell he was praying.

In the sick bay Minns lay stripped on the operating table set up in the centre of the cabin. Leather straps bound his body to prevent him moving with the pitching of the ship; they would also stop him fighting against any loss of effect from the anaesthetic. Matthews had arranged instruments, bandages, swabs and stitching gut in a neat array inside a glass locker where they would be safe and at the same time easily available. He stood by the table, waiting to administer the anaesthetic.

On the other side of the cabin Tim Goodwin had been propped up in his bunk with his back against the bulkhead. He could overlook every stage of the operation. He shuddered under the fever frequently, but his eyes were bright with drugs and he bathed his streaming face continuously with a large towel.

They waited to feel the movement of the ship change from sudden corkscrewing to steadier pitching. It would be the best they could hope for. A messenger knocked on the door and called out, 'First Lieutenant's compliments, sir. We are steady on new course and Coxswain has the wheel.'

'Very good.'

Strong wore uniform trousers with just a vest, to give maximum freedom of movement. His feet gripped the deck in rubber-soled slippers. In spite of the cold, his face and bare shoulders glistened with sweat. He had forced all extraneous cares and thoughts from his mind so that he could concentrate solely on strict obedience to Goodwin's orders. He needed implicit faith in his own ability to withstand the tremendous strain.

Minns gazed up at him without expression; then, as though sensing Strong's tautness and as if in answer to his Captain's mute appeal for a sign of trust and confidence, he smiled and his body relaxed. His voice barely reached the watching men. 'Don't you worry, sir. I'm not. You'll do a right good job on me, I know.'

His eyes closed and Strong looked at Goodwin. The doctor nodded and Matthews pulled back the white sheet covering Minns' body and plunged the hypodermic into his abdomen.

Telephones rang and voice-pipes were filled with talk as galley rumour raced round the ship.

The operation had begun.

4

Tim Goodwin stared down at Minns with a strange mixture of cynical indifference and despair. If only he could control the bouts of trembling, reduce the fever heat burning up his face and head with such intensity. More than anything else, he wanted to spare Strong the ordeal ahead — a simple enough operation for a doctor, and one that really did not require a surgeon. However, for a layman it would be a hideous experience. Minns would not suffer nearly as much as the Captain.

He began to feel a little light-headed and recognized the symptom as his principal danger. Drugged as he was, it would be too easy to let his mind break the chains of will-power to roam freely, even wildly. Once that happened he would be letting down Strong — and somehow the Captain was more important to him than Minns. *Steady,* he told himself, *it's already happening.* Once he started treating Minns casually he would be useless to Strong.

He wondered why Strong and Matthews were looking at him with such startled expressions, and quickly realized he had spoken aloud. He shook his head, wiped the sweat from his face and heaved his thin body more upright in the bunk. 'Sorry, I'm all right now.' He said it with what was supposed to be a reassuring grin. In fact, it was a ghastly, grotesque imitation which filled Strong with foreboding.

The doctor's voice was a mere whisper as he said, 'Put the rubber gloves on, sir. That's better. Scalpel.' He watched Matthews hand the slender, wicked-looking instrument to the

Captain. 'Now find a point on the abdomen two-thirds of the way in from the right hip bone downwards along an oblique line.'

Confused by the sudden arrival of the moment he had been dreading, Strong looked dazedly at the instrument placed in his gloved hand. The doctor's instructions, muttered with much obvious effort, barely registered in his shocked mind. It was Matthews who traced a disinfected finger across the white flesh until Goodwin gestured weakly.

'That's it. We call it McBinney's Point. Make an incision there and draw the blade down obliquely towards the abdomen for four inches, no, five — that will give you more space to work in.'

The words struck Strong with the impact of sharp pain. He looked away from the wide-open eyes of the patient, feeling that he must be sick if he saw them again during the operation. Ridiculously, the many discussions of appendicitis cases at sea flashed through his mind. Then, they had been theoretical; now, the practical application of the many views he had heard had fallen upon him.

Hands — they were not his, could not be his, because they seemed to be working without conscious control — pressed the scalpel against the piece of flesh still bearing the livid imprint of Matthew's finger. Goodwin raised a limp arm and shook his head. Strong was swept by sudden panic. What had he done wrong already? Then the doctor's low voice steadied him.

'Don't be frightened to press hard. Quick, down hard.'

Strong jabbed and felt momentary surprise at the ease with which the scalpel slid through the flesh. Matthews had drawn the line of incision and now the layers of fat fell apart as the blade cut downwards. It came out with a slight tug, and, while the sick-bay attendant busied himself with swabs, Strong glanced at Minns with an apology ready on his lips for the pain he must be causing. Minns managed the faintest of smiles which said what the Leading Seaman could not — probably would not — say: that he trusted his Captain.

Goodwin's irritated mutter broke the silence. 'Get on with it. He can't feel a thing. Look hard at the wound and you will see the abdominal muscles. They run in lines down and across, meshed. Cut them between their lines.'

Strong could see the muscles glinting redly, crisscrossed like lines of insulated wire. There was no feeling through the rubber gloves as he put finger and thumb inside the wound and sliced the scalpel through the lines of muscles. Then he nodded at Goodwin.

'Good,' whispered the doctor. 'Now for the peritoneum. It's quite a large translucent tissue with lines running down its length.' Goodwin was dripping with sweat, forcing himself to concentrate. 'Divide it, sir. Pull it apart between the lines and you'll see the intestines. They will bulge through the opening in the peritoneum.'

Good God, thought Strong, *why can't the fellow talk in English?* But his fingers were working quickly, if clumsily, as the doctor spoke. The tissue parted and sure enough a messy substance oozed through. He looked at it with amazement, fascinated despite himself.

'Look down it, sir, and nearby, outside the line of the incision, you will see a large intestine, much larger than the rest. You won't miss it. Everything's going fine.'

Strong probed again, found the intestine and tried to expose it. A sinew impeded the groping and Matthews, still controlling the bleeding, handed him a pair of scissors. He pulled at the sinew, slipped in the scissors and cut. Without knowing it, he pulled at the patient's nerves and searing pain beat down through the anaesthetic and flowed through the body. Strong was startled at the low moan that hissed through Minns' tightly shut lips.

Matthews was white with strain as he reached to a shelf for a bottle of alcohol to bathe the skin round the wound. Then the ship reared up and rolled. He stumbled and fell back against Goodwin, who began cursing fluently; while Strong lurched forward over the operating table, his arms outstretched to steady himself on the far side. Blessedly, he avoided landing on the open wound with its exposed confusion of nerves and muscles.

As Matthews groped for support, the bottle fell from his hand to smash on the deck. Without fuss, he found another and carried on with his duties. The ship righted herself and they braced themselves against the compensating roll in the other direction. Minns wriggled on the table, but the anaesthetic had regained control of the pain.

There was an uneasy silence in the small cabin. Goodwin began tossing about against the bulkhead, holding his head in his hands and shaking it violently to ward off the dangerously wild dreams closing in about him. Matthews and the Captain gazed at him horrified. Not now, not at this stage...

Goodwin pulled the sodden towel from his face and looked back at them. Then a shadowy grin twisted the corners of his slack mouth. 'My God, you two look a damn sight worse than I feel.'

Strong looked down at himself. The clean white vest was hanging limply wet and suddenly his trousers seemed heavy with the amount of sweat they had absorbed. He brushed an arm across his forehead and sighed with relief.

'Now, got the caecum yet?'

Strong's face was blank, and Goodwin waved a hand impatiently at him. 'The large intestine — found it yet?'

Strong shook his head and probed deeper to the side of the cut.

'Look for the white bands running down lengthways like ribs. Think of a gigantic gobstopper — bull's-eye, I think, is the correct term.'

Goodwin seemed to be enjoying himself now, but the old fear had returned to Strong. Then he saw it, a raw, red lump of flesh with white sinews running down its length. 'Got it, Doc. But for God's sake, hurry.'

'Right. Follow it downwards to the end and the big lump of flesh attached to it is the appendix. It'll be a bit green and yellowy.'

Carefully, Strong parted the muscles, tracing the white lines downwards. There it was, the rotten appendix, exposed at last. He must have threaded through another nerve, for a second groan came hollowly from Minns. He snatched his hand away from the cut and a scream of shocked pain pulsated across the cabin.

'Hurry,' Goodwin croaked in alarm. 'Pull it out and cut. No, wait. Matthews, give Minns another shot of procaine. Hurry, man.'

Strong stepped back while Matthews filled the hypodermic and administered the second dose. Minns opened his eyes to silently thank him. His body relaxed.

'Right. Get cracking, sir.'

Strong bent over the patient again, beads of his perspiration falling in tiny spatters on Minns' stomach. He put a finger and thumb into the wound, gripped the appendix and pulled gently. Surprisingly, it gave easily and he was able to slip the scalpel underneath and cut it clear of the intestines. With a gesture of disgust, he threw it into the bucket of dirty swabs.

Grant and Guns crouched with Masefield behind the windscreens on the bridge. They watched apprehensively as the seas broke over the bows. Every pitch had to be judged to see if some slight alteration of course would reduce the movement even a little. In the wheelhouse the coxswain drew upon thirty years at sea to signal any tendency of the ship to swing off course a second before it happened. The wheel whirled under his hands, backwards and forwards, correcting the swings. *Concord* shuddered as the rudder fought the sea. Above all was the wind, not yet at full force but singing through the rigging with sufficient noise to make Masefield shout every order.

The engine-room telephone rang and Guns lifted the receiver from the wheelhouse bulkhead. 'Bridge.'

'Engine room here. Murray speaking. Who's that?'

'Guns here, Chief.'

'What's the news, Guns? Operation finished yet?'

'No. There's been no word. Number One's here. Do you want him?'

'No. Just wanted to know what was happening.'

Guns replaced the receiver and joined Masefield on the port wing. 'That was Chief, Number One. Wanted to know if there was any news.'

'My God, I wish there was. Wonder how much longer this business will take?'

Guns shrugged impassively, then suddenly a wave, larger than the rest, raced in from the starboard bow. Masefield shouted at the coxswain, 'Watch that one to starboard, Coxswain.'

Concord lifted with a jerk and heeled over under the impact while the helm fought to control the threatened spin. It was too late. She rose to the crest, listed to port and unexpectedly rolled to starboard before sliding down the wave while veering off to port — a corkscrew which could prove fatal to Minns.

The sudden movement threw Strong forward without warning, and this time he fell across Minns with one arm jabbing into the white flesh of the belly, pulling at the side of the raw operation. Goodwin had been supported by the bulkhead for the first roll and pitched forward by the second. He was pulling himself erect again while Matthews withdrew a bleeding hand from the hole it had made in a glass-fronted locker when he automatically plunged it towards the bulkhead for support.

Minns had been the least affected. Immune to pain since the second injection, he had watched the antics of the three men with astonishment. He had seen Strong fall across his body and had winced in anticipation of the pain. Instead there had been no feeling; he had hardly felt even the Captain's weight.

Matthews went to work without orders. Clean swabs, soaked in disinfectant, wiped at the flesh soiled by Strong's clothes. Goodwin had gathered control of himself and began to give his next instructions. He stopped when he saw Strong's face. It was white, strained, and quite unexpectedly Strong rushed to a corner of the cabin to be sick, violently sick.

Matthews handed him a glass of water which he drank in deep gulps. Then, with a muttered apology to no one in particular, he returned to the operating table, his eyes red-rimmed.

'It's all right,' whispered Goodwin. 'No harm's been done. All's well, so far, sir. This is the tedious part. You have to sew all those cut tissues and muscles together, one layer at a time. Matthews will show you how.'

In the Leading Seamen's mess Bill Gridley sat silently at the mess table watching another sailor playing solitaire. Half an hour had gone by since the word passed round that the Captain had started the operation on Minns. There had been an abnormal silence in the mess, broken only by furious curses when the ship pitched or rolled more than usual. It was nearly time for the afternoon watch to go on duty, and already various hands were putting on oilskins and duffel coats, eager for the bosun's mate to pipe them to their sea-duty stations where they could keep abreast of news from the sick bay.

The solitaire player threw down his cards and got to his feet, scowling. 'What the hell is all this about anyway? You bloomin' idiots are behaving as though the King of England was dying or somethin'. What 'appens if Minns packs up anyway? We'll all probably be dead tomorrow, accordin' to the number of ruddy U-boats around.'

Gridley walked over to him slowly and stopped with his face thrust close to the other's. 'You shut yer big face, sailor. There's a man up there who's worth an 'undred of you. Yes, it's the Captain I'm talkin' about. The good Lord'll look after Minns, and if He chooses to let 'im live, it'll be the Old Man who will 'ave put a word in 'is ear. So you shut yer face and siddown until we hears somethin'.'

Eight bells announced noon, and the watches changed. Boland and Harry Prentice relieved Grant and Guns on the bridge, but the latter pair refused to go below until some sign came from the sick bay. Masefield kept command of the ship with the coxswain staying at the wheel. Even Boland could not find it in him to treat the matter with his usual cynicism. He sensed the tension in Masefield.

'How long now, John?'

'Oh, hullo, Peter. The Old Man's been at it for the last forty-five minutes. Should be over soon, please God.'

Strong fumbled with the last layer of muscles. His hands and legs were beginning to tremble but doggedly he persevered with the needle and gut, sewing crudely but effectively at the elusive tissues. Matthews gave the wound a final swab and clipped the edges of skin together. He handed a fresh threaded needle to the Captain, who, after a slight pause, slowly sewed along the five-inch cut while Goodwin closed his eyes and gave himself up to the ravenous fever.

It was done — over and finished. Strong stood erect, looking down at the patient, who throughout the last fifteen minutes had been snoring fitfully. Though exhausted, he helped Matthews carry Minns to the bunk and then lifted Goodwin in his arms while the attendant remade the doctor's bed. They laid him down gently, pulled the covers over his thin, burning body and bathed his face with fresh water. He opened his eyes and glanced at them both. His voice was still weak, but the words came clearly to Strong.

'All right, sir. Don't you worry, he'll be quite all right … did a good job … both of you.' Then he shut his eyes and trembled fiercely.

Strong looked at Matthews for a moment and held out his hand. It was all the reward the one-time nurse wanted — in *Concord* it was generally considered that praise from the Captain was worth almost any medal you could mention. Then Strong stumbled from the cabin and stood on deck, taking in great gasps of fresh air, ridding himself of the stink of anaesthetic and rotten flesh. When clean, bitter Atlantic air had washed his throat, he climbed to his cabin, lay down fully clothed on the bunk and lifted the cover of the bridge voice-pipe. Masefield's hoarse voice answered.

'Bridge here, sir. First Lieutenant speaking.'

'Good, Number One, resume our station in the escort. The operation is over, and only God knows whether it will succeed. Doc seems to think everything's all right. Send a signal to *Firefly* telling her it's all over. I'll come up after I've had a rest.'

'Aye, aye, sir. And from all of us, congratulations, sir.'

Masefield sounded relieved and cheerful and, as he lay back, Strong thought it must be the first time since they had sailed that Number One had seemed so breezy. Already he was slipping back into his role of Captain. A few minutes ago he had dealt with the physical pains of a Leading Seaman; now he wondered how to deal with obviously mental burdens of the First Lieutenant. *It must be family trouble,* he decided. *Worst of marrying a pretty girl; they've always got someone else after them, and that leads to only one outcome — trouble. Must have a word with Number One.*

Then he gave way to nausea.

Leading Seaman Bill Gridley was at his action station at 'A' gun on the foredeck when the news flashed round the ship that the operation had finished and Minns was going to be all right. Matthews had let it be known that he would be up and walking in a few days.

Gridley sucked hard at a boiled sweet and in a loud voice over the wind told his gun's crew, 'There yer are, see? I told yer everything would be all right. We got a bloody good skipper, and Number One's OK too.' He exuded good cheer and wellbeing. 'Yessir, on the 'ole our bloomin' officers ain't so bad. You got to 'ave officers in the ruddy Navy, so I suppose we got better than most.'

He showed splendid indifference to the chuckles of derision that followed.

5

Dinner in the wardroom was like, according to Chris Sterling, trying to eat fish and chips on a rollercoaster. Six days had passed since the operation on Minns and the first warnings of approaching storms, six days in which they had become accustomed to the constant buffeting and high-pitched whine of the wind. Even Strong was beginning to believe that the optimists were right, that this was the worst they would meet this trip.

Then another signal shattered the illusion. Masefield was attempting to gulp down bacon and eggs — only simple meals had been possible for everyone for too long — when the bridge messenger knocked on the wardroom door and handed him the signal.

'Captain's compliments, sir, and will you have everything movable battened down.'

The signal read: 'In areas south of Greenland and westward to the United States eastern seaboard winds will reach gale force by tomorrow afternoon. Cyclones moving eastwards are expected to reach these areas…'

He handed it back to the messenger and returned to his meal, announcing at the same time, 'Now we know this isn't the worst. Looks like gales, gales and more gales. What's the fuel position, Chief?'

Ian Murray was imperturbable as usual. 'Fair enough, if you chaps don't start roving about the ocean looking for trouble. Should have about eighty tons in hand if we keep up this speed.'

'Been out on deck recently, Chief?' Masefield was grinning and, behind his expressionless mask, Murray was glad. The First Lieutenant had been behaving strangely seriously since leaving Liverpool.

'Not for a while, no. Why?'

'You ought to. Plenty of excitement, and there will be plenty more. It's quite tricky negotiating the upper deck in sea boots. Slide all over the place.'

'No, thank you,' replied Murray fervently. 'I'm not the sort that craves excitement.'

Boland broke off a muttered conversation with Prentice to intervene. 'You seem to be enjoying this weather, Number One. Must say it makes a pleasant change to see you so cheerful again.'

Masefield was still smiling. 'Well now, Peter, do you think there could be some reason for it?'

With such an opportunity, Boland could hardly miss. 'Not that I can think of, old boy. But it amazes me how you go on leave one day and come back the next looking and behaving like a frustrated spinster. Now you revert to the old gay quip and cheerful smile. Must be a reason, but it beats me.'

'My leave seems to worry you, Pilot. I've told you before — mind your own bloody business.' The words came quietly, yet forcefully. Boland shrugged them off.

'That's most unkind of you, John. I've got your best interests at heart and it worries me no end to see you constantly miserable. I know what it is — loneliness. That's what it is. Best sedative for that, old boy, is work; lots and lots of lovely hard work. It helps most men to forget the most dominant of all problems today.' He paused to emphasize his meaning and enjoy the silence that had fallen across the wardroom. 'You know what I mean — unfaithful wives and sweethearts.'

Most of the wardroom had guessed at the First Lieutenant's anxiety about his wife, but this was the first time it had been mentioned publicly. Distaste for Boland mingled with curiosity. Masefield finished eating and carefully placed knife and fork together. He looked at Boland before speaking in an even, measured voice. The stewards were outside in the pantry; the officers had the wardroom to themselves.

'I'm speaking on equal terms now, Boland. Rank doesn't enter into this. Someone has to say it, so it might as well be me. You are a bastard — a troublemaking, vicious bastard of the worst possible type. I could sit here for hours and describe all the sorts of bastard you are without repeating myself once. I'm not saying this because of your interest in me — or is it Sonia? — but because the Navy is saddled with you and, more particularly, this ship.'

Even the Chief Engineer was grinning with enjoyment of the scene. But his good sense made him speak. 'Well, you two have got it off your chests. Perhaps we can live in peace from here on. Can't have bickering in the wardroom, you know. Bad for morale. Suggest you both forget it.'

Masefield nodded, but inwardly he was fuming at himself for permitting Boland the opportunity to goad him to this extreme. The Navigator was eating impassively, smugly satisfied at the result.

'I'm going on rounds of the mess decks to see that the ship is battened down,' Masefield said to Murray. 'Will you report the engine room secured to the Captain, Chief?'

'Right, Number One. I'll see to it in a moment.'

When the First Lieutenant had left, the doctor collapsed on the anteroom settee, his cheeks pallid and his lacklustre eyes like blue basins. The fever had died days before, but the torment of seasickness plagued his tired body.

'How are you feeling, Doc?' asked Prentice.

Goodwin muttered his reply. 'I shouldn't be here, should never have submitted to that stupid urge to join the glamour boys in uniform.'

There was a general chuckle of sympathy. Boland, still purring at his technical victory over Masefield, turned on Goodwin.

'Want a priest, Doc? A good Catholic like you should have mumbo-jumbo read to him before he passes out, isn't that so? The beads — why not count beads? They might take your mind off it, m'boy.'

Murray scowled. 'Lay off it, Pilot. The Doc's having a rough time.'

'That's not the point, Chief.' Boland was enjoying himself. 'The point is that as a Catholic, Doc might as well take this purgatory with a smile. All Catholics have to go to purgatory some time. They buy themselves out of it with hefty contributions to the Church before they die. Sort of religious blackmail. Doc can't have been dishing it out to the extent he should. That's the trouble.'

There was a mild titter from the others and Goodwin raised himself on an elbow. 'Don't worry, Chief,' he muttered resignedly. 'He knows I can't help defending the Church every time this argument crops up. So he baits me — a great baiter, aren't you, Boland?'

'Nonsense, m'boy. I'm just trying to find out why, when you are lying there feeling bloody awful and I'm here feeling just fine, you should think your God any better than mine.'

'It's not your God I object to, it's the way you worship Him,' Goodwin replied shortly. 'It's your religion that's at fault.'

'Why? Fifty million Protestants can't be wrong, surely.'

'Why not?'

'Why not, indeed. M'dear boy, we are fairly tolerant and not really hidebound with bigotry. Neither do we have Virgin Marys, beads and crosses littering the place like you people — that's plain, unadulterated idolatry.'

'Have it your own way, Boland. But at least it gives us faith, and there's damn little of that in you.'

The Navigator grinned ironically. 'Faith, m'dear chap. What's that? A god that half a dozen other religions deny, including your own? Man can't even make a snail, a worm or a toad, yet he creates gods all over the shop. Believe me, Doc, gods die just like the miserable people who create them. Then what? Another Messiah comes along, and when he perishes another Pope claims to be the one and only true disciple. No, thanks. I don't want that sort of religion or faith, whether it's yours or mine. Mine comes in useful when forms have to be filled in. That's all.'

Goodwin was quietly content. He had revealed Boland for what he was — a brittle pseudo-sophisticate with a philosophy as shallow as himself, aimed, of course, at the gallery.

Chief was angry at the malice underlying the exchange, and took advantage of the pause to interrupt. 'Pete — Doc. For heaven's sake, we've had enough unpleasantness for one night. Let's have a truce.' He looked balefully at them both. 'I'm senior to both of you, and I can get quite bloody-minded when driven to it.'

Harry Prentice seized the opportunity to take the Chief's side. 'You see,' he said with a bored expression to Sterling, 'even our seniors and alleged betters behave like children at times.'

Murray left the wardroom and clambered up the ladder to the Captain's cabin below the bridge. Strong looked up at him in surprise when he knocked, and beckoned to the one chair in the tiny space.

'Sit down, Chief. What brings you to deck country at this time of night?'

Murray sat in the chair, took a packet of cigarettes from his pocket and offered one to the Captain. Strong shook his head, and the Chief took his time in lighting his own. Then he broke the silence.

'Two things really, sir. First is about fuel. How bad is the weather going to get?'

'I don't know, Chief. About as bad as you and I will ever see, I should think. Why?'

'Well, at present speed, and if it gets no worse, we will have about eighty tons to spare. But if it really gets bad and we have to heave to for long, or make any large diversions from our course, then we will probably be eighty tons short.'

'Yes, I've already been thinking about that. But there's nothing we can do for a day or so. It may die down a bit. What's the second problem?'

Murray shrugged forward in the seat and stubbed out the half-smoked cigarette. 'Can I speak unofficially, sir?'

'Of course, Chief.'

'Well, there's trouble between Boland and Masefield. They had a pretty bad quarrel tonight and it's not good for the wardroom. Youngsters like Prentice, Sterling and Grant are hearing things they shouldn't.'

'Was it about Masefield's leave?'

'Yes, sir. Boland's getting under his skin deliberately and openly hinting that his wife was unfaithful to him.'

Strong sighed and gulped at his cocoa. 'I was afraid of this. Number One has been trying to forget by working too hard. He'll crack up if Boland goads him beyond a limit. There's nothing much I can do about it. I'll have a word with Masefield tonight. And thanks, Chief. Don't worry. I'll be diplomatic about it.'

Murray lumbered to his feet, said goodnight and went below to his own cabin, thankful that the one man who could bring peace to the wardroom happened to be Strong. The Captain had already guessed at a much deeper reason for the row between Masefield and the Navigator; a reason that lay far beyond the wardroom, beyond the ship.

Masefield knew that Boland wanted his wife; and Boland knew now that Sonia Masefield was free for the taking.

A few minutes later, Strong staggered to the bridge and joined Grant and Guns in the wheelhouse. Not long afterwards the First Lieutenant arrived to make his report. 'Everything secured and battened down, sir. The mess decks have been warned and Chief has told his chaps in the engine room.'

'Very good, Number One. How about depth charges?'

'Well lashed down, sir.'

'Good. If it gets much worse, Guns can have the primers removed. We don't want those things breaking loose and exploding under our stern.'

Grant broke in, 'Just had a call from the radar operator, sir. He says it's broken down and he is trying to trace the fault.'

'Very good, Grant.'

Masefield became suddenly aware that the Captain sounded very weary. The usually wide, steady eyes had narrowed to thin slits with the merest flicker of a gleam shining behind the almost closed lashes.

'How about fuel, sir? Chief told me we had about eighty tons in hand.'

'That's if we can keep this up,' replied Strong grimly. 'If we have to heave to then it might get serious. There won't be much chance of fuelling at sea. Incidentally, how's our fair-weather sailor taking it? Sterling, I mean.'

'He's an odd bird, sir. Eating like a horse and, although looking a bit pale, he's not been seasick to my knowledge.'

'Good. I'm going below to my cabin. Come down for a minute.'

Strong gave instructions for the watch to Grant and left the bridge, followed by Masefield. Once in his cabin, Strong beckoned the First Lieutenant to sit in the same chair that had been occupied by Chief and began talking as he discarded oilskin and duffel coat.

'Hear you had a row with Boland in the wardroom this evening. Number One.'

'Yes, sir.'

'Well, stop it. You of all people should know better than to allow quarrels to break out into the open at sea, especially among officers. Bad for all concerned if the troops hear about it, and they always do. I know all about Boland and in future, Number One, avoid any open breach with him, at least for the present. Is that clear?'

'Yes, sir. I'm afraid I did lose my temper.'

'That's all. I'll see you in the morning watch. Goodnight.'

'Goodnight, sir. I'm sorry about that scene.'

Strong grunted and Masefield left the cabin smiling inwardly at the thought of Chief acting as peacemaker. But of course he had been right to bring up the matter with Strong. He should never have risen to Boland's bait so easily.

By dawn, the gale-force winds promised by the Admiralty were screaming through the rigging and around the superstructure with frightening fury. Masefield and Sterling peered intently through their binoculars, trying to brush aside the mist, rain and spray while maintaining a semblance of station on the few merchant ships in sight. They would be the rear of the convoy; at least, they hoped so. There were three of them, two to port and one to starboard, and they heaved and wallowed with fearful slowness.

In calmer days they had looked what they were — ten times the size of *Concord* and almost yeomanlike in their massive solidity. Now they were being tossed about disrespectfully by a sea that cared little for size.

Sterling, who had recoiled at being in rough weather in a small boat, seemed to have found the wild challenge of the storm an invigorating experience. He had not complained, nor did he appear frightened or unduly worried by the dismal prospects that lay ahead.

'Signalman,' called out Masefield suddenly, 'call up the nearest of those ships on the port bow and see if she answers. I want her dead reckoning for our position at 0800.'

'Aye, aye, sir.'

'Messenger, call the Captain, Lieutenant Grant and Mr Bellows. And tell the chief bosun's mate I'd like to see him before the hands are piped to breakfast.'

'Aye, aye, sir.'

At 8 a.m. Grant and Guns relieved Masefield and Sterling. The four officers were formally exchanging information when Strong appeared, skilfully balancing a cup of tea in one hand while supporting himself with the other. He had been on the bridge most of the night, and Masefield noticed that for the first time he had not shaved.

'What's the signalman doing?' he asked abruptly.

'Trying to call the nearest merchantman to port, sir,' replied Masefield. 'I thought they might give us a position we could check against our own.'

'Good idea. Grant, see that the signalman keeps trying to raise him for a bit longer.'

Grant was looking very white and unsteady. The well-set-up young body suddenly seemed flabby and flaccid. He nodded, and Masefield put a hand on Sterling's shoulder.

'Come on, Sub,' he said. 'Let's get down below and see what sort of breakfast is going.'

Bill Gridley was an immovable rock in the chaos of the Leading Seamen's mess. Amid a rushing swill of water, spilled tea and stale breadcrusts, he was anchored firmly to a long wooden bench as he addressed his mates.

'You got nothin' to worry about. I'm tellin' yer, I've seen storms that would make this bastard look like the first breath of spring. And I'll tell yer another thing. If it gets any worse there'll still be nothin' to worry about. Any man that could fix up old Minns without knowin' a bloody thing about the knife can take this old bitch to hell and back.'

His mates were still unused to this open worship of the Captain by an old hand reputed to dislike all officers on principle. O'Flynn shook his head, puzzled, and murmured as though to himself, 'By the Holy Virgin, it just beats me, so it does.'

Futile attempts to maintain the zig-zag had ceased; in any event, it was unlikely that U-boats could operate offensively in those seas. It was all *Concord* could do to keep the three merchantmen in sight.

After nearly an hour of intermittent flashing, the signalman brought a feeble reply from the nearest merchant ship. It looked as if the reply was being made by torch, and frequent mistakes made reading difficult. When the message was eventually deciphered, Strong was not surprised to find that the difference between the two estimated positions was negligible. Whatever other faults Boland might have, he could be relied upon to keep an accurate check on *Concord*'s position.

By now Strong was convinced they had parted with the convoy. The three ships ahead had lost contact with the ships in their respective columns and *Concord* had religiously maintained station on them. He could not risk breaking R/T silence to call *Firefly* and it seemed pretty certain that the leader would not call them until he was sure the convoy was out of danger or that the rear ships had drifted off course.

It was shortly after noon on the 24th and Boland had made another check on his dead reckoning position. As Strong left the bridge, he called out to the Navigator, 'This is one Christmas Eve we won't have to worry too much about U-boats. Can't imagine Jerry leaving the peace down below to surface in this blasted weather.'

Kapitän zur See Kurt Cassel ducked down behind the conning tower bulwarks as another monstrous, white-capped peak bore down on *U-114*. With him on the conning tower were Lieutenant Franz Wout, a signalman and two lookouts. They were secured in their positions by steel chains clipped round their waists. Fair-haired with a round, youthful face — he was only twenty-six — Kurt Cassel squeezed his small wiry body into a corner and cursed the accident off the American coast that had wrecked his electric motors and made it impossible for the submarine to dive. Worse, all torpedoes had been fired.

He had been heading for the Bay of Biscay and home, a dangerous voyage for a U-boat on the surface, when the storm caught up with him 500 miles from Newfoundland. For three days the slender ship had struggled mightily to survive the terrible pounding from the seas; the submarine would not ride the crests like an ordinary surface craft, but tended to cut into and through the great walls of water. Yet Cassel, soaking wet, unshaven and suffering from a chronic lack of sleep, felt confident that *U-114* could survive if the weather grew no worse.

A lookout shouted, 'Dark shape on port bow.' The last word of the report was screamed above the wind and the German commander, tensed and ready at the instant, focused his glasses on the merchant ship ploughing through the curtain of rain and spray not more than a hundred yards away. She was a frightening sight, charging down on them, one second rearing her huge bows into the air and in the next plunging down into a trough with a surging roar.

Cassel shouted his orders down to the control room and *U-114* strained to alter course against the power of the sea, away from the urgent danger of collision. The engines turned faster and the propellers threshed frenziedly. It was too slow. Horror struck at Cassel as realization dawned that they could never make it, never escape from the menace of this ship.

Franz Wout yelled in his ear, 'For God's sake, what will we do?'

In that curious way the mind often registers odd thoughts in moments of stress, Cassel thought how strange that Party Member Franz Wout should appeal to God at that moment. He was a Nazi, and in Cassel's judgment the Nazis had turned their backs on God. Thank heavens he had never joined the Party and learned how not to die. He would go down with *U-114* as his father had gone down at Jutland, with honour and faith.

They were his last thoughts.

A minute before the collision, *U-114* was sighted from *Concord*'s bridge. Boland sounded the alarm bells and the astonished crew scrambled to their action stations. Strong rushed to the bridge and took in the scene with a glance. Collision was inevitable. He calculated the U-boat's chances and coldly congratulated the merchant ship's captain for maintaining a ramming course. It took guts to risk a ship in this sort of weather.

He called out to Masefield, 'Get the men off the upper deck, Number One, before they get washed overboard. Tell a gun's crew and the depth-charge party to stand by. Remainder get below.'

But the crew were reluctant to leave the deck as the final scene in the life of the U-boat was being played out. They huddled behind protective shelters and watched, fascinated.

'Why doesn't he dive?' Boland shouted excitedly.

'Probably can't, for some reason,' Strong replied without lowering his binoculars. 'Must be; they're abandoning ship. Bloody fools. No one can live in this sea.'

Only a few yards separated the two vessels, and tiny black shapes could be seen leaping from the conning tower to vanish in the turbulent sea. Then Masefield yelled, 'Look at their commander!'

Cassel was standing wedged behind the conning tower's machine-gun mounting. He was facing the towering merchant ship with his right hand dramatically saluting. He disappeared from sight as grey, solid steel bows crashed down on *U-114*. A rasping roar, like prolonged thunder, grated above the noise of the storm; the merchant ship writhed in quick, jerky motions as she ran right over the submarine, which appeared briefly just clear of her stern.

It was upside down and the propellers were turning idly in the wind. A wave washed over her, pushing her down under the weight of water. When it passed, there was no sign of *U-114* or anything to show that for a fleeting moment in the storm-ridden lives of the *Concord*'s crew the enemy had come and gone so tragically.

Strong felt suddenly sick. He should have cheered when the U-boat went down. But somehow the speed and awful certainty of the enemy's fate had nothing whatever to do with war, and therefore appalled him.

Boland's voice brought him back to the present. 'There's something wrong with *Clan Forbes,* sir. Someone's waving from the bridge.'

All eyes now focused on the merchant ship, which had turned broadside on to the sea. 'Good God!' shouted Masefield. 'She's going to break her back.'

A prayer welled up inside Strong. There was nothing he could do to help; to approach close to the obviously damaged ship would be too great a risk. He wondered how seriously she had been crippled by the collision and guessed that the U-boat had ripped a gash in her bottom.

The *Clan Forbes* was listing over on her side alarmingly and the figures of her crew could be seen running along the slanting decks to the lifeboats. There was a frantic effort to get at least one boat in the water.

A terrible rending of steel and the snapping of girders reached them above the wind, and *Clan Forbes* sagged visibly amidships. Her holds filled with water, bursting the welded seams as her back cracked under the strain. Someone shouted, 'Look, they've got a boat away!'

Sure enough, a small lifeboat was being washed clear of the stricken ship. Then a wave caught it and turned it beam on to the next, which hit with awful ferocity. The lifeboat was tossed almost completely out of the water and, when the wave passed, it fell thirty feet, turning a full somersault as it toppled downwards. Men were flung out and not seen again; all that remained was an occasional sight of the boat's upturned bottom.

Three sharp cracks split through the wind, and eyes were switched back to the *Clan Forbes.* Her stern had gone, her bows pointed skywards. Two men could be seen scrambling from side to side of the slanting foredeck with dreadful, comical absurdity. There was no way out for them and they must have known it. Yet they continued to run and stumble as though safety must lie close by. Their will-power broken, under the anaesthetic of panic they had gone quietly mad.

Silence gripped *Concord.* All hands watched with fixed horror as the cargo ship lurched once, then again, and finally slid stern first beneath the waves. In the second before the foredeck vanished, the little running figures met and locked each other in their arms. Like passionate lovers, they died in a last, comforting embrace.

The rising weather had claimed another victim and the wind howled as though in triumph. The hurricane was approaching its climax and in an hour it would be dark — Christmas Eve. The Midshipman, on watch with Boland, cried out, 'Captain, sir. We've lost the other two ships. There's nothing in sight.'

'What about the radar?'

Boland sprang to the radar-room telephone. 'When will the set be ready?'

'Not yet, sir. Haven't traced the fault.'

'Will you ever be able to repair it?'

'Don't think so, sir. It's a shore-repair job.'

Boland replaced the receiver and shook his head at Strong. 'Nothing doing, sir. They think we will have to wait until we reach harbour.'

Strong grunted. 'Right. We'll break R/T silence. Pilot, call up *Firefly* and ask her for a course to rejoin the convoy.'

Boland nodded at Prentice, who picked up the radio telephone, pressed the button and began calling, 'Swallow calling Seagull, Swallow calling Seagull.' He released the button and stood listening. There was no reply. 'Swallow calling Seagull, Swallow calling Seagull.'

The telephone remained stubbornly silent. Strong looked at him for a moment and said, 'Keep on trying, Mid.'

He pressed the receiver against his ear and listened intently. A confused jabber of voices sounded very distant.

'Swallow calling Seagull, Swallow calling Seagull.' He repeated the code names desperately. Again there was no reply. He replaced the receiver and looked at Boland for instructions.

The Navigator turned to Strong. 'Shall we keep trying, sir?'

'Yes, every five minutes for the next half an hour. We will check our position now, Pilot, and set course for St John's. With the radar still out of action and the R/T dead, it's about the only thing we can do. Messenger.'

'Yes, sir.'

'Tell the Engineer Officer I'd like to speak to him in the chartroom, please.'

'Aye, aye, sir.'

Boland followed Strong into the chartroom and the two were still bending over a chart of the North Atlantic when Murray knocked on the door and came in, his overalls drenched by rain and spray.

'Chief, we seem to have lost contact with the convoy, radar is still out of action, and we can't raise *Firefly* or anyone else for that matter on the R/T. I'm setting course for St John's. How about fuel?'

'Less than two hundred tons, sir. Enough for about five days' steaming.'

'Good. I think the full weight of the hurricane will hit us tomorrow, perhaps tonight. That will last for about two days, then we get the calm centre to run through, say about six hours. After that, another day or two of pretty bad weather and that should be the end. We'll keep at our present speed, Chief, and we can pray we don't have to heave to for long.'

Chief looked grave. 'It sounds pretty tight. There'll be nothing to spare for emergencies, sir.'

Strong gazed at him thoughtfully. 'No, Chief. Nothing at all.'

6

Christmas Day, 1942, was the day the galley closed down. It was no longer possible to keep pots and pans on the stoves or to keep the fires alight. Only the electric plates could be used to make cocoa and tea. With cooking abandoned, the cooks set to work making enormous mounds of sandwiches — cheese sandwiches, Spam sandwiches, cheese sandwiches, Spam sandwiches.

In the wardroom pantry, the same sandwiches were made by the stewards and a large pot was lashed on the electric cooker and kept filled with steaming cocoa. Ropes were laced through the wardroom chairs and officers came down from the bridge to eat while still in their soaking clothes. There seemed no point in changing. Water had entered the ventilating shafts and poured in streams into the mess decks, cabins and wardroom. There was no hope of stopping it. It had to be endured.

Boland, the Chief, Doc and Mid sat round the wardroom table looking dolefully at their Christmas dinner — a plate of sandwiches. Each was intrigued by the movements of the mustard and pepper pots which sat in wooden frames in the centre of the table. One big roll and they would catapult out and fly across the room. They would do nothing to stop that happening; they were only morbidly curious about which direction the pots would take. Doc reached out for another sandwich.

'Seasick, eh?' snapped Guns in mock anger. 'With an appetite like that you must have tapeworms.'

Doc looked down at his plate. It interested him only as long as it stayed there. If it suddenly disappeared to the deck, he would do without one. Despite the lashings, the chairs moved about quite a bit with every roll and tipped dangerously at a heavy pitch. Boland complained bitterly that no stomach could be expected to hold down a sandwich if it was subjected to constant lunges in almost every direction.

'Holy Moses, Doc. Say you had to pull an appendix out in this stuff. That would be really something.' It was Sterling, taking time off from stuffing down sandwiches to consider medicine without a qualm. His fellow officers glanced at this one-time timid young man with new interest. It seemed that quite unremarkably he had become a sailor and an officer — they would all readily admit that he had always been a gentleman.

'Funny,' he continued between munches, 'but all the appendix operations I ever heard about always took place at sea in rough weather. Why is that, do you think, Doc?'

Goodwin looked at him hopefully. 'Probably because a minor illness like seasickness sets it going. How are you feeling?'

'Fine.'

'A pity; great pity.'

Harry Prentice roused himself to say, 'Incidentally, Chief, do you remember that pretty girl we met in the bar at the Adelphi one night in Liverpool about three trips ago?'

Boland had left the table to collapse in an armchair, where he would stay until his turn came to go on watch at midnight. He interrupted energetically. 'Women? Who mentioned women? I'm both interested and frustrated. Proceed, m'dear chap. You have my undivided attention.'

At that moment Strong walked in to join the picnic. 'You can forget all about girls. Here, Doc, Mid — a signal you can decode now.'

He was surprised when Boland left his chair to help the other two with the tedious business of deciphering. *Funny,* he thought, *how the man seems to be changing, really trying to work. Emergencies and an element of danger do queer things to people.* He reached out for a sandwich and smiled.

'Well, not too bad for Christmas Day. After all, it might be ship's biscuits in another week.'

There was a groan from Chief, and Strong looked across at him. 'What's the matter, Chief? Food not elaborate enough?'

'No, that's not it, sir. It's the thought of another week of this. I'd give a lot for some firm, immovable earth under me right now.'

'How's the engine room? Flooded?'

'Just about, sir. Gets any worse and I'll keep the whole department down there and reduce the watches. The off-duty men can sleep in some warmth there. Saves using the upper decks.'

'Good idea. Barometer seems to be steadying a bit.'

Concord lurched heavily and Chief raised his eyebrows. 'I'd call it a liar and throw it overboard, sir.'

Boland changed chairs to sit closer to Strong and Chief. He looked sombre, as though he had been trying to stave off some terrible disaster but instead had been caught in the mesh of events. His eyes betrayed an inward excitement that warned Strong of the approach of something the Navigator considered important enough to worry him. Boland's voice was low, disturbed; and in quick surprise Strong detected a note of hysteria.

'There's something I'd like to ask you, please, sir.'

'Yes, go ahead, Pilot, get it off your chest.'

'It's about what happened yesterday, the *Clan Forbes* and that submarine. I've been plagued with nightmares about it ever since.' He raised his eyes and looked directly at the Captain. 'You see, sir, I believe it was murder.'

His breathing was heavy, as though the effort had cost him much. Chief stiffened and glanced anxiously at Strong, who sat with head bowed and eyes averted.

'Is this important to you, Pilot? Important enough to keep me off the bridge?'

Boland's eyes gleamed angrily. 'To me, yes. But then perhaps I'm one of those peculiar people who think this war bloody senseless, all war for that matter, and recognize murder when I see it.'

'Calm yourself, Pilot. I merely want to know if I can help. I haven't the time to become involved in a discussion on the theory of war. But if I can help you understand why the captain of the *Clan Forbes* rammed that U-boat then I don't consider that to be time wasted.'

Boland was not to be calmed easily. His face had become suddenly flushed and his voice vibrated with a passion none of them had believed existed in his usually languid character.

'I'm sorry, sir. But it had nothing to do with war. *Clan Forbes* could have got out of the way and that submarine was in trouble, a ship in distress. I know it. It was a cold-blooded murder.'

Chief said mildly, 'Take it easy, Peter. Our job, in fact everyone's job, is to sink U-boats. The skipper of the *Clan Forbes* may or may not have been able to avoid that collision. He didn't try because he knew that the storm had given him a chance to kill the enemy, so he took it.'

'And what happened? He murdered the crew of the U-boat and his own crew.'

Even Murray grew slightly red and irritated. 'He destroyed a U-boat. That's what counts. And since when have you been so bloody concerned about the fate of others?'

'I'm not. But I don't like seeing murder committed in the name of war.'

Strong looked from one to the other, then across at Goodwin and Prentice, who were listening while pretending to decode the signal.

'You know, it's funny, Pilot, but like Chief I would never have expected this to be brought up by you. But now that you have done so, you might think upon this: the captain of the *Clan Forbes* did a brave thing. But it was reckless and, as you say, he lost his ship and killed his men. He must have been impulsive and bitter to have done that.' He met the Chief's astonished eyes. 'Yes, Chief, I'll surprise you a bit more. Pilot is right, it was murder without reason. That submarine wanted help. But if it had to be sunk, we could have done it with gunfire, without risk.

'You see, you are trained and brought up to believe in destruction of property and life provided it is the enemy that suffers. Boland and I are not. I believe in the rule of survival at sea in which sailors, any sailors, help each other when ships are in trouble. The Navigator hates war and is revolted by unnecessary killing. Therefore, although we are all in uniform committed to one side, there is a difference in our approaches to it. And mine, Chief, is more closely allied to the Pilot's than yours.'

Chief frowned in consternation at an entirely unexpected side of the Captain being so readily revealed, while Boland looked at Strong in relaxed relief, all bitterness and passion expended in the effort to establish and confirm one of the few principles of life that had ever bothered him.

'Does that answer your problem, Pilot?' Strong went on dispassionately.

'Not quite, sir. But it will do. I had thought that this whole business had affected nobody, that I was the only one who gave a thought for those poor devils.'

The ship stopped dead against a wall of water. She quivered along her entire length, and tons of water rumbled swiftly down the foredeck above the wardroom, echoing like a kettle-drum. A stream poured down into the cabin flat and slushed into the wardroom. Strong grabbed another sandwich and hurried off to the bridge.

The signal had been decoded and Doc and the Mid rose to leave the table. The ship gave a quick, shuddering roll to starboard and, with a faint bleat, Prentice was thrown to the deck and slid down to the ship's side. Doc grabbed at the nearest support — the Chief's chair. Immediately unseated, Murray landed on his bottom and skidded down the listing deck to land on top of the Mid, who was picking himself up. The two collapsed again in a bundle of flying arms and legs. Doc, still holding on to the Chief's chair, fell flat on his face and lay there threshing about.

Boland gazed down at them in astonishment. 'Look,' he cried with a wide grin. 'A ruddy cabaret, *Concord* style.'

A steward left the pantry with a cup of cocoa in each hand, delicately balancing himself against the pitching and tossing with the contemptuous disregard of the professional for the amateurs scrambling about the deck around him. A heavy spurt of rushing water poured down the companionway and hit the deck at his feet. In slow motion, quite unhurriedly, his legs danced an involuntary jig, lifted uncontrollably high, and left him with no visible means of support. He landed with a heavy thump on the deck, the cups still clenched tightly in his hands, although the cocoa was now streaming down his white jacket. His face expressed pained, solemn astonishment.

Masefield followed the water down the ladder and surveyed the scene without surprise. 'Well,' he murmured. 'I've never seen so many playful kittens in a warship before. Having fun?'

Chief and the Mid unravelled themselves and helped the doctor to his feet. The steward vanished into the pantry for more cocoa, but his cursing could be heard through the serving hatch.

Chief slapped the back of his chair hard. 'Can't understand what the Yanks did with these chairs in rough weather.'

'Stuck them down with chewing gum,' guessed Sterling.

'Hmm. Might have to use that in the engine room soon. There's still some odd pieces of wire and machinery we haven't found a use for yet.' His face brightened. 'Perhaps they're storm stabilizers.'

'No,' replied Boland. 'Yanks never went to sea in rough weather. Had more sense.' He staggered back to his armchair. 'Oh, for a nice soft bed with black silk sheets and a hot wench to smother me. Bloody war! I'm wasting my young life.'

'You know, I think you're right,' groaned Murray.

'What?' said Masefield, laughing. 'Your young life? Come off it, Chief. You're a respectable married man. Plain wicked, that's what you are. A dirty old man.'

'Well, what's wrong with that?' said Doc, coming to Chief's aid. 'It's perfectly normal and a sign of virile youth to want to crawl into bed with a healthy woman. Even the Bible mentions it, quite frequently in fact.'

Harry Prentice decided to join in what promised to be the sort of casual flippancy he wanted to master. 'Women,' he snorted. 'Nothing but bags of trouble.'

Boland threw him a look of pity. 'So spake the wise old man of the East — East End, more like it. You are much too young for this sort of conversation, Mid. Just speak when you are spoken to and you might learn from your elders and betters.'

'No, Boland,' said Masefield with ominous softness. 'Let the Mid tell us how he found out about women. How he acquired this profound titbit of general knowledge.'

Prentice blushed and Boland laughed. 'Not a bad idea, Number One. Come on, Mid, tell us the story of your sex life. You can start with the old line: *'Twas a dark and stormy night and three men sat in a brothel. Bring us a dame, said one, and this is how my tale began.*'

Prentice strove to meet the challenge and the mood. 'Matter of fact, you are right. I had my first woman in a brothel. She was a German girl in Santos. At one time she had been kidnapped by white slavers.' He saw the incredulous looks around him and faltered.

'You're kidding, Mid,' said Masefield disbelievingly.

'No, I'm not. It's perfectly true. How could she have got to a Brazilian brothel otherwise?' He glanced around hopefully, but lost his nerve when he saw the light of glee and mischief in Boland's eyes. It struck him then that they were all laughing at him. Tears sprang to his eyes and trickled down his cheeks, and his lips curled as he tried to fight them back. Suddenly he bent down and sobbed with his head held in his hands. The sound of the hurricane was all that could be heard in the wardroom.

Masefield broke the awkward silence by saying with clear sincerity, 'Sorry, Mid. We shouldn't have pulled your leg, but you did ask for it, you know. Go ahead and bawl your eyes out. There's nothing to be ashamed of.'

Prentice wiped his face with a handkerchief and sniffed loudly. It was Boland, amazingly out of character, who went across and leaned over him. 'Mid, you may be still a boy, but to us you are a man carrying as much responsibility as anyone. We respect you, Mid, as long as you don't try to be someone you are not. Now let's have the truth. You have never had an affair with a woman, have you?'

Masefield thought the Navigator was leading up to some cruel twist and was about to intervene with a heated rebuke, but it died in his throat. Mid was looking up at Boland gratefully.

'No, never. I've always been frightened of women, and scared to admit it.' He stood up and walked over to the First Lieutenant. 'Lieutenant Boland is right, sir. I'll try to be my age.' He grinned and picked up the decoded signal. 'Shall I take this up to the Captain?'

Masefield looked at him wonderingly and nodded. 'Let me see it first.' He read the signal, handed it back to Prentice, who left the wardroom to report to the Captain.

'Wonders never cease,' the First Lieutenant muttered to no one in particular. 'That boy might turn out all right yet.'

The Chief interrupted his thoughts. 'What did the signal say, Number One?'

Masefield took a sandwich to a vacant chair and replied, 'It seems that we have been struck by a hurricane. The convoy has scattered and the Admiralty have requested news of us. Apparently they can get no replies from *Firefly*. No one knows where she is, where the convoy is, where the corvettes are or where we are.'

'That's funny,' said Boland. 'Wonder what's happened to *Firefly*?'

But Masefield had retreated behind his private thoughts. He was wondering what had happened to Sonia.

In the early hours of the next morning — Boxing Day — it happened. Great seas ran before the hurricane. Boland and the Mid, waiting impatiently for the end of the middle watch, saw a huge, white-streaked towering sea swerve in the wind and purposefully race towards the port side of the bridge. They were numbed by the fearful sight, unable to move or take any action to avoid it. The great wave shouldered the ship at masthead height with a thunderous roar.

Concord staggered under the mighty blow and began to rise up the wet, streaky wall of water. One minute Strong was sitting in his chair, dozing; the next second he was thrown to his feet and propelled through the open cabin doorway into the passage as a green flood poured in after him. He hurled himself up the bridge ladder in time to see the toppling seascraper gather, spread, and suspend itself momentarily over the bridge like a vast canopy.

Then it fell, beating men to their knees with its frightful force, tearing hands from their grips on solid objects and spilling them across the bridge. Slowly, *Concord* emerged from the flood, wounded but alive.

Dazed and drenched, Strong fought his way to the wheelhouse and took command while Boland looked for damage. The port side of the bridge was smashed into a mess of twisted steel; the heavy steel scuttle clamped hard over a porthole in Strong's cabin had been wrenched from its hinges. Water streamed through it into the cabin. The for'ard bulkhead opposite the porthole had been stove in by the force of the water jet.

At 0330 Boland recorded the damage in the log book and made the entry: *Met hurricane in position.* Under Strong's orders, the little destroyer reduced speed, turned into the sea and hove to.

Half an hour later the First Lieutenant and Sterling crawled up to the bridge to relieve Boland and the Mid. As they arrived, a startling crack pierced the night.

7

For a second there was some doubt about the cause of the crack. Then a shout from one of the lookouts swivelled all eyes at the foremast set abaft the bridge and just for'ard of the fore funnel. The slender few feet near the top were swaying loosely, pulled in one direction by the wind and in the opposite one by the weight of the aerial and stay wires. Without warning it leaned over, splintered at the break and crashed down to dangle dangerously near the signal yardarm.

Masefield reacted quickly. 'Messenger, call the watch and tell the chief bosun's mate to send a work party up the mast to cut away the topmast. Pilot, call the Captain, please.'

Two minutes later Strong joined the officers on the bridge. 'What is it, Number One?'

'Topmast has come down, sir.' Masefield pointed at the broken mast. 'If it breaks free of the wire stays, it will smash into the whaler and motor boat. We're trying to clear it now, sir.'

With only two lifeboats, a dinghy and the carley rafts, the motor boat was valuable. Below, in the well deck, the chief bosun's mate was mustering the hands and gesticulating at the swinging topmast as he assessed the chances of clearing it. The insistent shrieking of the wind, as it cut through every corner and cranny in the ship and whistled through the wire rigging, reduced hearing to the extent that in exposed positions even shouting was hopeless. With sudden decision, Masefield turned back to the wheelhouse and approached Strong.

'Captain, sir, I'd rather not send any of the men up that mast. They won't have a chance.'

Strong grinned without humour. 'I was wondering when you would think of that, Number One. We'll have to risk it coming adrift.'

Masefield called out to the messenger. 'Tell the chief bosun's mate to belay that last order. No one is to go up the mast.'

As the messenger vanished below, there was a heavy thud from behind the bridge. Masefield rushed out again and, in the murkiness, saw the broken topmast swaying against the fore funnel with the force of a battering ram. He returned to the wheelhouse and reported to Strong, 'The damn thing's bashing into the funnel now, sir.'

The Captain's voice was pitched just high enough to reach above the wind. 'Well, that's all right. There's nothing we can do, unless you want to change your mind again and send someone up. Better warn the Chief and wait until this eases down a bit.'

Masefield ordered Sterling to keep the Chief informed and stood hunched beside Strong. 'Much more of this, sir, and I think we are going to have to watch the crew. Some of them are getting worried.'

'So am I,' said Strong with feeling. 'But there's damn little I can do about it. What's our speed?'

'About four knots over the ground.'

'Then we'll just have to be patient, Number One. Even prayers might help.'

There was no dawn, just a gradual awareness that what had seemed so frightening at night was even more so when it could be seen. It was a world that none of them had dreamed could exist: a world of jagged green-and-white rocks, cliffs of water and rolling humps which dwarfed the tiny *Concord*. That it was all water did not matter. The nightmarish impression of having been transferred to some steamy, impossible world remained. The green-and-white scene looked as solid as concrete, as unyielding as steel.

The peaks of the waves were being whipped into a white, boiling frenzy of foam, much as a mountaineer might expect at the end of some storm-swept Himalayan conquest. *Concord* climbed the great waves, sometimes sluggishly, sometimes fast, until at the top she hung poised, neatly balanced, while on the bridge it was possible to look down into the turbulent valleys as much as a hundred feet below. Then she slid down with bows plunging beneath the water while buoyancy and weight fought for supremacy. At other times, she would swing wildly off course and roll dangerously close to the limit beyond which she must capsize.

The roll indicator in the wheelhouse gave sixty-three degrees either way as the maximum for safety. She had touched the red arrow several times already. There would be audible sighs of relief when she straightened up from these rolls and quivered to shake herself free of the depressing weight of the water.

Strong sat in the chair in his cabin with a foot of water sloshing about his ankles. He was indifferent to the bitter cold and the soaking wetness of his clothes and everything he touched. He was brooding on his ship and his men; for the first time in his career at sea he felt instinctively that this was the most dangerous hurricane of them all. Four hundred miles to go, fuel for four and a half days, and a maximum speed of three knots. How many days would they really last? He braced himself as the stubborn destroyer began another climb, a slow, straining climb which meant she would never reach the top.

On the bridge Masefield and Sterling ducked automatically as a thousand tons of water fell on the foredeck in a blinding, tumultuous roar and slapped hard against the bridge. Then she was through it and already plunging downwards towards the flat desert below. Rivers of water raked the decks, while overhead the long wispy trails of cloud rushed by, low and menacing as though hurrying to keep an undefined rendezvous over some other ocean. Occasionally they sprayed *Concord* with rain, hail and heavy flakes of snow.

There was little or no sleep for anyone. Damage appeared in the most unlikely places: water spilled through crevices, deck seams sprang apart under the constant strain. Only in the engine room was there heat. Here, the stokers worked and fired until relieved, when they collapsed at their stations, snatching at rest until their turn came round again. The lives of all aboard depended on three unpredictable slender threads — the engines, the rudder, and the skill of Louis Strong.

With Christmas already past, the inveterate gamblers among them were opening books on their chances of reaching port by the New Year and being taken up only by the optimists. The others wondered if they would reach port at all.

At 0800 Strong struggled up the bridge and heaved his weary body on to the Captain's seat. Lifelines were stretched along the upper deck and all traffic in the open had been stopped. The depth-charge crew huddled under what meagre protection was offered by the quarterdeck. They were nearing the end of the sandwiches taken with them, and they had not had a drink for twelve hours.

In many white faces could be seen the first signs of wonderment at the ferocity and protracted bitterness of the hurricane. Hidden behind half-closed lids, even the eyes of Louis Strong were revealing the faintest hint of fear, not for himself, nor really for his ship, but for his men. He knew there might well be worse to come.

Grant and Guns relieved the watch, and Masefield was about to follow Sterling down the ladder when he caught a beckoning gesture from Strong.

'Number One, I want the watch routines changed. From now on, all sea-duty watches are to be cancelled except the bridge personnel — lookouts, quartermasters and messengers. The depth-charge crew will have to take their chances in getting below. Guns can organize that now and see that all primers are removed. I want only one Officer of the Watch on the bridge and only for two-hour watches. I'll spend most of my time up here until we're through. Four hours is too long in this weather. We can't expect maximum efficiency for longer than two hours at a time.'

'Aye, aye, sir.'

'And, Number One, take yourself off the roster. I want you available to deal with any emergencies. See that Chief is told. He can reorganize the engine room as he thinks best.'

Masefield disappeared below, and Strong was about to turn round to speak to Guns, when it happened.

There was nothing anyone could do about it. The huge grey-and-white wave raced before the wind, dead ahead but swinging slightly across the bows, wider than the rest. It grew in height as it closed the distance, while *Concord* began a curious writhing motion in the foothills. Then it reared high above them, and for a second even the black scudding clouds were blotted out by the wind-whipped crest. It hit *Concord* with a slicing slap by the bridge, falling at the same time.

Strong, Grant and Guns were tossed into the port wing by the cascading torrent as it swamped into the wheelhouse and poured below. A lookout at the back of the bridge held firm to a stanchion and watched the wave wash down over the upper deck towards the stern. His eyes rested briefly on the trail of wreckage and then he ran to where the officers were clambering to their feet.

'Port whaler's been damaged, sir,' he called out.

Strong and Guns rushed to look down on the damage. If the motor boat which was stowed away underneath the whaler was also wrecked, it could be serious. It was clearly evident that if the motor boat had escaped it could never be launched until the wreckage of the whaler had been cut away.

The First Lieutenant and chief bosun's mate were ready to meet the emergency. The ship was already heading into the sea and wind, hove to. There could be no hope of reducing the movement. Nevertheless, they soon had a working party hacking away at the davit ropes with axes and throwing the broken spars overboard. The work had to be carried out on a steel deck less than six feet wide, with no guard rails outside the boats.

'Guns, stand by the quartermaster and see he doesn't let her swing off course too much. One more like that and the lot down there will go overboard.'

Strong's eyes were fixed on an additional danger to the repair party below. The loose steel topmast was still swaying with every roll. If it broke free of the wires holding it against the yardarm, it would fall among the men working on the whaler.

He saw the First Lieutenant break off a discussion with the chief bosun's mate to look up. Then the Petty Officer picked up an axe and small steel-cutting saw and began climbing the mast. Strong resisted the temptation to have him brought down. His voice would not carry down to the deck, and by the time a messenger reached the First Lieutenant it would be impossible to contact the chief bosun's mate, who would certainly turn a blind eye to any gestures. There was another point to consider: the example being shown by the chief bosun's mate would lift the spirit of the crew.

As the Petty Officer reached the yardarm and sat astride it with his legs locked underneath, *Concord* rolled to starboard with a jerking heave. It nearly unbalanced him, but at the same time swung the broken topmast towards him so that he was able to grasp the loose aerial and wire stays from which it was dangling.

The repair party below watched as they waited with the First Lieutenant to resume cutting away the wreckage of the lifeboat. The Petty Officer first hacked at the aerial with an axe, and after it parted he began pounding at the first of the thicker wire stays. He edged nearer the mast to get a better grip, unlocking his legs as he did so. *Concord* began a slanting roll to port — nothing unusual. She was heeling over heavily when Strong felt a sudden impulse to yell a warning. She was not coming up; instead she kept on listing further and further, until the yardarm was practically awash. One more mighty swipe with the axe and a wire stay that had been lying across the steel yardarm snapped apart. The broken section of the mast dropped six feet, caught the wind and catapulted through the air. One end of the wire curled round the Petty Officer's left ankle, pulling him outwards. His leg shot up at a strange angle and he toppled downwards, his hands frantically flailing in a desperate search for a grip.

His additional weight parted the second wire and, with a brief, hypnotic scream, he followed the broken mast into the sea. Both vanished in seconds, and the watching sailors gazed at the sea, shocked at the suddenness of the tragedy.

Masefield was the first to recover and, at his orders, the damage-repair party swarmed out again to attack the lifeboat. Two men climbed into the boat to cut the rope lashings and lowering tackle which had jammed. The destroyer rolled to port again and the sea washed past them, only inches away.

Grant saw the next wave racing across the line of the swell, wide of the starboard bow. He rushed to the back of the bridge and stood alongside Strong, shouting and waving at the men working below. His words were picked up by the hurricane and whisked away into the tumult which shrieked back at him malevolently. He hit his Captain on the shoulder and both men ducked low as *Concord* shuddered under the blow.

Masefield signalled with his arms and the working party dived for cover, all except the two men working in the boat itself. When the green torrent had washed down the ship, the wrecked whaler had gone — and with it the two sailors. They had never had the slightest chance of escaping; indeed, they must have known that by working inside the boat they had taken the almost impossible gamble that the sea would give *Concord* a respite.

This second tragedy within minutes of the first was too much for Strong. He turned and almost ran back to the wheelhouse, where he took his customary position hunched in his seat. No one dared to speak to him. The motor boat had been cleared of wreckage and could be used if needed. But at what a price! Strong was not even sure that if they had to take to the boats the motor boat would last for longer than a few seconds in that sea. Probably its only real value lay in the fact that it was intact and provided some psychological comfort to the men.

Masefield appeared at his side, bleary-eyed with tiredness and his voice almost hysterical as he made his report. Strong placed a hand on the young officer's shoulder.

'It's all right, Number One. I saw it all from the bridge. Nothing you or anyone else could have done. It's this bloody war, this bloody weather. There's going to be more of that sort of thing before we get through.'

Blinding anger swept through Masefield at the sheer futility of the incidents. Without realizing quite what he was saying or to whom he was saying it, he screamed at Strong, 'All for a bloody boat, d'you know that? All for a bloody boat. Jesus Christ, but the blasted thing wasn't worth one life, let alone three.'

They looked at each other for a moment while Masefield called on reserves of strength to bring himself under control.

'Now go below, John,' Strong said. 'Get some rest and something hot to drink. Then come up here and relieve me.'

Masefield smiled weakly, despairingly. 'I'll read a short service on the mess decks first, if you don't mind, sir. I'll explain that you can't leave the bridge.'

Strong nodded his approval and turned to Guns. 'What about the depth-charge crew, Guns? We'll have to get them off the quarterdeck and the primers taken out of the charges. Better start organizing that now.'

Masefield interrupted. 'Please, sir, I'd like to do that. Guns can warn them on the telephone to watch me. I'll keep an eye on the sea from the midships well deck, and when I give the sign they can leave the quarterdeck and make a dash for the mess decks.'

'All right, Number One. But for God's sake be careful yourself.'

For the next ten minutes they watched from the bridge as the men on the quarterdeck took advantage of the few seconds' lull between waves to remove the primers from the depth charges. Then Masefield exposed himself to the seas by standing well out on the wing of the upper deck, from where he could see how *Concord* was behaving. The larger of the waves seemed to have passed and subsided into a series of rough corrugations when he lifted his arm and waved. One by one, the six men on the quarterdeck stumbled along the upper deck, slowed down by the weight of their clothes and the cumbersome sea boots.

Then they were safe. Strong relaxed and let a feeling of thankfulness sweep through him. At the same time, he decided to have a word with the First Lieutenant. He was taking too many chances. Sonia, of course, and Boland.

Two more days passed, and even the most optimistic had given up expecting a New Year's Day in harbour. The wardroom was in a shambles. Masefield, Boland, Doc, Sterling and Guns huddled in corners or wedged themselves into immovable furniture. Nearly everything in sight had been lashed down or broken. In the pantry the stewards were cutting the last of the sandwiches. After today there would be no more bread, and precious little of anything else. In the main galley the stokers and 'Chips', the carpenter, had rigged up a metal frame on the electric stove in which a huge cauldron fitted. It could be kept about one-third full of either hot water for brewing tea or cocoa for the night watches. If filled at any higher level, it just spilled out.

Masefield was squatting on the deck between the fixed bulkhead settee and the wine locker. The wardroom carpets had been taken up and stowed in a cupboard. Water swilled around him but he paid it no heed.

Boland looked up impassively at the First Lieutenant and said, 'Rotten business, all this, John. A pretty bloody awful experience altogether.' He ignored Masefield's unintelligible grunt and went on blandly, 'Still, there is one consolation for you. At least it takes your mind off other things — and people. Sonia, for instance.'

He watched Masefield with a wicked light in his eyes. When the First Lieutenant reacted he wilted, scorched by the look of sheer hatred. Masefield had been fighting against waves of sleep; now he burned with fury. The cigarette he had been holding loosely in his right hand dropped unheeded to the deck, where it was quickly reduced to a floating mess.

He climbed to his feet with considerable effort, leaned against the roll of the ship and staggered across to the chair in which the Navigator was lying outstretched. His face was an expressionless mask from which only the eyes glinted redly as he stared down at his tormentor with rigid intensity. Boland tensed, waiting for the blow he was sure must come.

Masefield trembled slightly and the searing sensation at his temples died. He muttered distinctly to himself, 'The son of a bitch isn't worth it.' Then he stumbled from the wardroom.

The words hit the Navigator with an impact that hurt more than any physical blow. He could have taken that with a laugh; in fact, had often wondered if Masefield could be forced into striking him. But the unspeakable contempt and pure pity in the First Lieutenant's voice had penetrated the veneer of sophistication, stripped off the protective crust of nonchalance and laid bare a hidden core of tremulous uncertainty.

He had once told a young reporter, 'Secret of this job, m'boy, is to take everything in your stride. People are bloody rude, but if you make up your mind that no one can insult you then no one ever will.'

Masefield had done what many people had wanted to do for a long time. He had insulted Boland and the insult had struck home with force. Boland was intelligent enough to understand how Masefield had felt, and knew it had been as though

Number One had decided to tread on an insect and then changed his mind because even insects and lower life, like Boland, had the right to live.

The Navigator turned away so that the officers who had witnessed his complete degradation should not now see the self-pity, self-hatred and chagrin lurking in his eyes.

The old year of 1942 passed into history; the New Year came into the present with no abating of the hurricane, no sign that the relentless elements might relax their grip on the waning strength of *Concord* and her crew. The intention of the storm to wipe them out became brutally clear. For twenty days it had raged, playing havoc with morale and stretching the resistance of the weak to breaking point.

Ordinary Seaman Bradley Randall was one of the weak. He would one day inherit wealth. But somewhere in the past his aristocratic ancestors had intermarried and laid the shallow seed from which he had sprung.

He sat on a locker on the mess decks, his face pale, his eyes wild. 'My God, I can't go on,' he shouted hysterically. 'They'll make me go out there, I know they will. It's my watch and they will come and make me. I can't go out there.'

O'Flynn had neither patience nor sympathy. There was plenty of excuse for him; he had put up with the outbursts of young Randall since the storm first broke.

'Stop yer ruddy wailing, will ye?' he shouted back. 'Bejesus, why don't ye buy yourself a bloody aeroplane and fly yerself back to dry land? Sure and ye 'ave the bloody money.'

Bill Gridley was passing through when he heard the last of the exchange. He stopped and put a large, calloused hand on the youngster's shoulder. 'Nah then, sonny. Don't you listen to that ignorant Irish bastard. 'E ain't got no sense, no proper feelings like I 'ave. You're in my watch, ain't yer, so you won't 'ave to go on deck fer some time. Wot yer do is get some sleep and when it's time to go on watch yer comes with me, see? Ye stick close to Uncle Bill, boy, and nothing can happen to yer. And if I see ye right through this lot, sonny, why, ye won't forget me when this bloody war is over, eh? You with all that bloody money and a rich old man; why, son, we'll get on right bloody well, we will.'

The now bewildered Randall nodded his thanks and Gridley sneered triumphantly at the flabbergasted O'Flynn. 'That's me boy,' he chuckled hoarsely. 'Your friends will look after ye. Not like some of the ruddy Irish trash around 'ere.'

O'Flynn had been the accepted 'guardian' of the youngest member of the crew since he had joined. Gridley had known that the Irishman was using this to extract money and promises for the future from the kid. He didn't mind this state of affairs, but he had been looking for an opportunity to usurp O'Flynn and, as he put it to himself, 'get a ride on that gravy train meself'.

He swaggered off to his own mess before the enraged Irishman fully realized that a serious attempt had been made to poach his preserve, to entice his future stake from under his wing.

An ear-splitting, cracking thud echoed through the mess decks, bringing men to their feet in sudden alarm. A few minutes later the wet figure of the bosun's mate came running in from the bridge shouting, 'Fire! Fire party muster in the engine room!'

8

The First Lieutenant and Chief were directing a party of stokers sealing off an area between the for'ard generator and bulkhead, against which a barrel of dirty, oily waste was blazing, as the first of the fire party tumbled down the ladder from the upper deck. The urgency was self-evident; on the other side of the bulkhead was the ammunition locker.

Two hoses were connected to water valves on the lower level of the engine room and run to the second level where the fire was threatening to spread.

'What caused it, Chief?' Masefield yelled above the din.

Murray shook his head. 'The welding's split along that seam and a leak from the ammunition locker must have set the generator sparking. It wouldn't take much to set that lot of waste alight. Some of it's soaked in fuel oil and paraffin.'

The coxswain was in charge of the fire party and Masefield beckoned him across. 'Coxswain, send a couple of men to the ammunition locker and damp down the other side of that bulkhead.'

Chief looked at the sailor playing a stream of water on the shut-off generator. 'Number One, that chap over there, it's Minns, isn't it?'

'Yes, Doc's passed him as fit. Says any man who could survive the Captain's clumsiness is destined to survive anything. Anyway, he needs the sick bay for the rest of the sick report.'

Chief grinned appreciatively. 'The Old Man ought to take on Minns as a personal servant. He could show him off to guests.'

He broke off and looked with horror at the bulkhead. It was glowing red in patches. 'Good God, Number One, look at that bulkhead. The generator shorting must have caused another short in the ammunition locker.'

Masefield was already running up the ladder on his way to the threatened compartment. The hatchway was on the main mess deck, and as he burst through the blackout curtain from the upper deck, he grabbed the nearest sailor and ordered, 'Get up to the bridge and tell the Captain there's a fire in the for'ard ammunition locker.'

The man looked scared, but ran off to carry out his instructions. The two men sent by the coxswain to prevent a fire in the locker were standing by the hatch, playing a hose down into the red glow below them. Volunteer helpers were quickly donning asbestos fire-fighting suits. Masefield pulled one away from a startled sailor and began putting it on over his uniform. Then he took the hose and climbed down into the locker.

He saw the cause at once. A thick metal tube protecting the electric cables running from the engine room to the ammunition hoist was glowing with heat from the wires burning inside. That, added to the heat from the fire in the engine room, had given a false impression of the extent to which the ammunition was endangered.

One of the men had followed him down and it needed only a sign from Masefield for him to understand what was required. As the First Lieutenant climbed back to the mess deck, a messenger arrived from the engine room to report the fire under control.

Masefield reported to Strong on the bridge that both fires were now being dealt with, and arranged over the telephone for Chief to supervise shoring-up of the cracked bulkhead.

The Captain said nothing when it was over. He simply nodded his head and went below to his cabin. For a moment Masefield wondered if he was about to give way under the constant strain of command. Then he dismissed the thought and considered the Navigator instead. What was Boland after? Did he really think he could get away with it, an affair with Sonia? He answered the unspoken question himself: yes, the woman would fall for Boland, no doubt of it, and the thought filled him with possessive jealousy. She was his wife — and despite his determination to hate her, he recognized incredibly that he still loved her.

Sterling lay in his bunk, wet and miserable. It was the cold that worried him; yes, he could feel the cold. He thought of his home, the large white-painted Georgian mansion a few miles from Manchester, away from the smoke and filth of the industrial city. He remembered the different reactions the news of his appointment to *Concord* had aroused in his parents and Julie, the girl he had always regarded with brotherly affection.

His mother (solicitous, cloyingly so): *Take care, dear. If you ever get wet, have a hot bath and dry yourself well. Heaven knows what food you will get. And darling, don't do as sailors do when they call at foreign ports.*

His father (thankfully): *About time ye went out in the world, son. Do ye good, this war. And don't pay any attention to your mother. Drink a bit and sow your wild oats with the women — if they'll have ye. Learn to live, if you've got the brains — and I doubt that ye have. Don't ye worry about after the war, son. I'll look after ye, but take care of the brass. Don't ye spend too much money.*

Julie (the vicar's seventeen-year-old daughter): *I'm very proud of you, Chris, but I am going to miss you, honest. I'll write every day if you promise not to go out with other girls.*

He remembered her quick kiss and the dawning realization that perhaps she didn't like being treated as his younger sister. Strange emotions began worrying him. Like the Mid, he had not yet possessed a woman. The first stirrings of sex came to Christopher Sterling in the middle of a hurricane, in a small cabin already under water.

Julie seemed to change in his imagination. He saw her differently now, because he was growing up under the tension of the hurricane. She became an attractive young woman with long legs, high breasts and appealingly red lips. He liked the odd sensation and instantly recognized it for what it was. He gazed at the dripping deckhead and murmured softly, 'Julie, darling.'

He thought she would like that.

A buzzer sounded three times on the bridge and Harry Prentice called down the voice-pipe to the wireless room.

'Bridge.'

'Bridge, distress signal from *Firefly,* sir. Reads, "Have been holed in collision with merchant vessel. My position. Require urgent assistance."'

The Mid repeated the message to Strong, who came instantly alive and leapt to the chartroom, where he began calculating the distance between the leader's position and their own. He whistled to himself as the full extent to which the convoy had been scattered became apparent.

He made his way back to the wheelhouse and rapped out fresh orders. 'Port ten … full speed both engines … eighty revolutions. Midships … steer 240.' He crossed to the engine-room telephone and spoke to Murray. 'Chief, *Firefly*'s broken radio silence to send a distress signal. She's been holed in a collision. Now her position is well ahead of us and slightly to port. I've altered course and put the sea on our starboard bow. We'll try 120 revolutions at first and see if she can take it.'

'Right, sir,' replied the Chief. 'But we'll have to watch the fuel. I reckon there's not much more than a couple of days left in us.'

'*Firefly* hasn't got that long, Chief,' Strong said curtly, and replaced the telephone. 'Signalman, tell the wireless room to send the following to *Firefly* repeat Admiralty, SNO St John's, C.-in-C. Western Approaches and Captain D, Liverpool: "Am proceeding at ten knots to your assistance. ETA 1430 stroke 3." That's all. Messenger, tell the First Lieutenant I want to see him.'

'Aye, aye, sir.'

Concord was liking neither the alteration of course nor the increase in speed. She swung off to port persistently as the waves buffeted against her starboard side and the wind beat down on the superstructure, blowing her southwards. The quartermaster at the wheel fought the off swings with the rudder, struggling to keep her steady. She shuddered frighteningly under the increased speed and pushed her way through the water instead of trying to rise above the waves.

The First Lieutenant reached the wheelhouse looking alert. The story of *Firefly*'s plight had already passed round the ship. Strong greeted him crisply.

'Number One, *Firefly*'s in trouble about forty miles away. I reckon we'll reach her about 1430 if we can maintain this speed. When we get to *Firefly,* I want all hands ready. Lord knows what we shall be able to do, but everyone will have to be ready. You can warn the hands now. I've sent down for the Navigator and he'll be busy until this is over. So will you. The rest of the officers will have to rearrange the watchkeeping among themselves. I don't mind who is up here with me. And have Doc prepare the sick bay. Never know who might be, or might get, hurt.'

The numbness of the last two weeks was leaving Masefield, and he marvelled inwardly at Strong's vitality. The Old Man hadn't had a decent sleep for twenty-odd days.

The engine-room telephone buzzed. The Mid answered it. 'Captain, sir. Engineer Officer would like to speak to you.'

'Right. Chief? Captain speaking.'

'About the revs, sir. Can you take a bit more speed?'

'Might. Not much, though. Why?'

'It would be more economical if we could increase to 130 revolutions, sir.'

'Very good, Chief. Make it 130, then.'

He had just replaced the receiver when the wireless-room buzzer summoned an answer. The Yeoman of Signals answered and called out, 'Message from *Firefly,* sir. Begins: "Careful how you cross the road. It's not safe out here."'

Strong, who had met the crisis as though freshly rested, felt an attack of despair. He knew the leader well enough to understand that the flippancy implied urgency. He studied the sea ahead and mentally registered *Concord*'s behaviour under the pressure of the new speed. 'Mid, tell the coxswain to have the quartermasters relieved every thirty minutes and to take over himself at 1415.'

It was a wise decision. Keeping the destroyer even approximately on course was draining the strength of the helmsman. Masefield returned to the bridge and stood back watching the Captain, his affection for this aloof, reserved man overcoming his anxiety.

He moved forward to stand beside Strong and, more for something to say than because it was important, he asked, 'Shall I cross-check Pilot's dead reckoning, sir?'

'No, Number One. Pilot's doing a good job. Don't disturb him. I've told him to alter course as he thinks fit.' Strong looked round at Masefield. 'You know, Number One, I'm surprised at you. Boland's been getting you down, but you mustn't let it interfere with your work, or his. He's lazy, yes. But he's also pretty careful in this sort of emergency.'

'You're right, of course, sir. I'm sorry I said that.'

'Forget it. But now we are on the subject and there's nothing much that we can do at present, care to tell me what happened to make you break off your leave?'

Masefield's face went suddenly hard. He returned Strong's steady look and then turned away. The words came without effort. 'Yes, all right, sir. Why not? I discovered Sonia was being unfaithful, having an affair with some chap.'

'You are quite sure of this?'

'Yes, walked into the flat and found them in bed together.'

'That's proof all right. About the best.'

Both were silent, Masefield feeling sick and at the same time thankful that at last he had been able to unburden himself to the one man he respected above all others.

'Why are you allowing Boland to get under your skin so obviously, John?'

'He's guessed the truth, sir. And I know damn well what he is thinking. Next time he goes to London he'll ring Sonia, and somehow the thought of Sonia and him together revolts me.'

'Surely they deserve each other? No, don't get angry, John. You know, a man with Boland's background and experience can spot the playgirl type a mile away. You and I are children with women when it comes to his sort. And after all, if that's what Sonia is then you are better rid of her sooner and not later. Another thing, John. I don't believe Boland would do what you think. He's a bit of a *poseur* and likes acting — can't help it, in fact. But he is changing. Since we left Liverpool he has become a different person; not obviously, but in small ways. He's learning that there is no room for *poseurs* in war; that he is likely to be exposed at any time and it isn't worth it. Humiliation is worse.'

Masefield listened with growing astonishment. It seemed incredible to him that Strong should feel like that about Boland. As far as he was concerned, the Navigator was as much a bastard as ever. He shrugged and replied offhandedly, 'Perhaps, sir, but it's still not a nice thought and I'm afraid I've seen no change in Boland at all. I just can't stand him.'

'In that case, there's nothing I or anyone else can do to help, John. Time, I suppose, is the only cure. When this trip is over, we'll go ashore, have a drink and talk some more about it. Meanwhile, keep personalities out of your dealings with the Navigator. That's an order.'

Masefield smiled grimly. 'Yes, sir.'

Talk died naturally as thoughts switched to *Firefly* and her plight. Boland came into the wheelhouse and reported to Strong.

'Not making as much speed through the water as we hoped, sir. Won't get there much before 1500. Wind's taking us pretty far to the south.'

Strong sighed.

'Well, it's taking *Firefly* in that direction as well. Better bring her round to 250 degrees. Incidentally, how long at this speed would it take us to reach St John's?'

'Two days, sir.'

'Chief says we've got fuel for one and a half. We may have to pump oil overboard to get the survivors off *Firefly*. If we use the half a day's steaming for that and radio St John's for a tug to tow us in, we shan't need more than the extra day.'

'Tight fit, sir,' said Masefield uncertainly.

'It is, Number One. Got a better idea?'

At 1415 the coxswain took the wheel and Masefield left the bridge for a tour of inspection in the fore compartments. *Concord* had taken tremendous punishment; she had sprung leaks, even cracked a few plates. Chief had already reported leaking seams in the ship's side in the engine room and the fore bulkhead which had split during the fire was beginning to bulge round the shoring timbers. Only the fact that their course was still more or less into the sea had made the diversion at all possible.

Strong straightened his back as Boland gave fresh instructions to the coxswain. 'What's the matter, Pilot? Drifting too much?'

'Yes, sir. If *Firefly* has been hove to, I reckon she should bear about 220 degrees now. I've altered course to 255 degrees and estimate we should sight her at 1500.'

Strong nodded approval as the wireless-room buzzer sounded again. He crossed to the voice-pipe. 'Yes, what is it? Captain speaking.'

'*Firefly* again, sir. She says: "*Concord* bearing 050 degrees, range nine miles. No reply R/T or radar signals. Suggest you steer 250 degrees..."'

Strong shouted to Boland: 'Bring her back to 250, Pilot. What else, wireless room?'

'"Your help needed urgently" ends message, sir.'

'Right. Not bad, Pilot. She's got us on her radar now. Send down for the First Lieutenant, please.'

As Masefield arrived, Strong called out, 'Number One, we might have to pump oil overboard and launch a boat. I'll manoeuvre a lee and the oil will give some protection.'

There was no need for Strong to go into further details.

At 2.30 p.m. all eyes on the bridge were straining through the mist for the leader. He would have to be ahead somewhere; there could be no question of a prolonged search with their critical fuel position.

It was nearly 3 p.m. when Boland said in a quiet voice, 'There she is, sir. At least, I think so.'

Strong peered intently along the line, fine on the port bow, on which Boland's glasses were fixed. He saw a dark blur gradually taking on the faint outline of a ship. A lookout confirmed the sighting.

'Dark shape red ten, sir,' he shouted.

It was *Firefly,* less than a hundred yards away. A signal lamp blinked from the leader's bridge. 'Welcome, *Concord.* What delayed you?'

Strong grinned appreciatively. 'Yeoman, reply: "Well, well, another stray lost in the storm. How badly are you hurt?"'

He brought *Concord* ahead of *Firefly* and hove to, not daring to create a lee by lying broadside on to the sea unless and until it was absolutely necessary. The Yeoman reported: 'From *Firefly,* sir: "Mortally. Man your R/T."'

The atmosphere of cheerful relief at finding *Firefly* changed immediately. Sounds died away and on the bridge they could sense the grim resolution reflected in Strong's face.

'Reply, Yeoman: "My R/T and radar broken down. Suggest you send over survivors in boats."'

Firefly was now clearly distinguishable. Her bows were ominously low in the water and she was listing alarmingly to starboard. It seemed good sense to Strong that if possible it should be *Firefly*'s oil and boats that should be used, particularly if she was about to sink.

The Yeoman read out the reply as it was being sent. 'From *Firefly*, sir: "My boats wrecked and no power for pumps. Can you spare fuel oil?"'

'Tell *Firefly*: "Can spare fifty tons. Will start pumping under lee and send across motor boat and whaler."'

He read *Firefly*'s answer almost as fast as the Yeoman. The leader doubted if his ship would survive the next fifteen minutes. She was holed badly for'ard of the bridge on the starboard side and again on the starboard side of the engine room. He beckoned to the Mid.

'Go below and tell the First Lieutenant to hurry with the boats, Mid. Motor boat to tow the whaler, understand?'

'Yes, sir.'

The Yeoman reported another signal from *Firefly*. '"Thank you for coming. We are going rapidly by the bows but you are not to indulge in reckless heroics. One ship lost is enough. Your boats should come along starboard side amidships. Bless you."'

By now *Concord* was turning beam on to the seas about fifty yards from *Firefly*, protecting the latter from the full force of the waves. Chief was on deck directing the fitting of oil hoses to deck valves and, at a word from him, precious fuel oil began spurting over the port side. Gradually a thin film of oil spread across the rough surface of the sea between the two ships. Within minutes it became a visible layer, lying heavily on the sea, smoothing it out by its own weight.

Firefly was sinking lower in the sea when Strong ran to the rear of the bridge to look down upon the working parties on the upper deck. The starboard whaler had been manhandled across the waist between the funnels and was about to be dropped with the boat's crew already at their stations. As the motor boat swung out, he was startled to see that instead of the usual crew it was being manned by Masefield, Sterling and Prentice. He knew that the First Lieutenant intended not to order the men into the boats but to call for volunteers, but this … three of his officers!

At a signal from Masefield both boats were slipped simultaneously while the Mid tossed a towrope at the whaler, expertly caught by the bowman. Masefield swung the wheel and started the engine as the boat landed on the crest of a swell and was washed clear of *Concord*'s side.

He focused his binoculars on *Firefly* and saw men lining up amidships. Her starboard side was already awash and her end could not be more than a few minutes away. The leader was alone on the bridge, looking down at the gathering of his men as though assessing how many could be rescued by the two boats.

The crews of both ships watched the two tiny boats fight their way across the gap. The motor boat was being thrown about by the swell and drifting wildly off course. The weight of the whaler on tow was proving a mixed blessing; acting as an anchor it prevented the motor boat being carried away in the sea, which, in turn, made progress difficult.

Strong returned to the wheelhouse to keep *Concord* from being swept down on the stricken *Firefly*.

Masefield calculated his chances of getting alongside *Firefly* without being smashed against her. He could see her crew placing rope fenders over the jagged edges of steel which might tear the motor boat apart. He glanced quickly over his shoulder from the cockpit and saw Sterling and Mid huddled in the stern with casting lines, and thanked God that they had followed him unhesitatingly when he announced his intention of taking charge of the rescue operation himself. Grant had been there then but, for some reason, had held back with head averted.

Masefield had forced the motor boat to turn into the sea now, so that both boats lay parallel with *Firefly* and were being borne towards her by the wind and swell. Without the thick, pacifying layer of oil to calm the fierce threshing of the sea, both boats would have capsized the moment they hit the water.

Thirty feet separated him from *Firefly*. Sterling and Mid threw their lines successfully first time, and Masefield felt the boat being pulled alongside by willing hands crowding the destroyer's slanting deck. There was a violent thump as the motor boat hit a fender and he shouted, 'Twenty men now. No more.' An officer waved in reply and he resumed the fight with the controls to keep the boat from being smashed.

A voice penetrated the noise of the hurricane: 'Right, motor boat. 'Way you go. Bear off, and for Christ's sake, hurry.'

He spun the steering wheel, let in the clutch and opened the throttle full. The engine whined and the small propellers raced to grip the sea. For an eternity it refused to move, then sluggishly the bows turned out from *Firefly* and pointed more or less in the direction Masefield hoped to go.

He looked astern and saw the whaler jammed with men and her crew pulling at the oars to help ease the weight of the tow. *Concord* had been blown downwind towards them, narrowing the gap. But the strain was proving too much for the motor boat; they were making little or no headway and the whaler was only a few feet from the sinking *Firefly*.

Suddenly the boat surged ahead and the First Lieutenant brought her into the sea. There was a confusion of shouting behind and he leaned over the side to look back. The tow had parted and the next wave lifted the whaler high before throwing it hard against *Firefly*'s side. The rescued men and the boat's crew were tossed out into the sea as it splintered and capsized. Masefield covered his eyes in horror. Then he vomited and returned to the task of saving the handful in his own boat.

On *Concord*'s bridge an electrician reported to Strong as he gazed down on the scene of terror that had followed the loss of the whaler. Some of *Firefly*'s men had panicked, and the faint sound of shrieks and curses carried to him faintly.

'Captain, sir. R/T's working now.'

For a moment he missed the significance of the report. It reached through the shock in his brain and he jumped across the bridge to grab the telephone. '*Firefly, Firefly, Concord* here.' He waited tensely for the reply. When it came, the leader's voice was even, unhurried.

'Hullo, Louis. So your R/T is repaired just in time, eh?'

Strong cut him off and almost yelled into the instrument. 'I'm sending the boat back, sir. For God's sake come off yourself.' He released the speaking button and listened to the leader for the last time.

'Sorry, Strong. It's too late now. She's going fast. Bless that motor-boat crew and bless you. No time to chatter any more. Goodbye, Strong, and don't forget to see my wife.'

As he stopped speaking, Strong saw *Firefly* lean further over to starboard and submerge slowly. Her bows vanished and the sea rose to the superstructure. Her officers had joined the leader on the bridge and the men crowded on to the quarterdeck. Then the watching crew of *Concord* heard it; it rose high above the howling wind, across the rearing of the sea, a last defiant chorus sung lustily and without a quaver:

'Bless 'em all, bless 'em all,
The long and the short and the tall.
You'll get no promotion
This side of the ocean,
So cheer up, me lads, bless 'em all.'

The motor boat had been hoisted inboard and Masefield sat still in the cockpit listening to the sturdy voices. He heard sobbing behind him and turned to see Grant leaning against a davit with tears coursing down his cheeks.

From Strong downwards, the men of *Concord* recognized in the song from that group of men about to die on *Firefly*'s quarterdeck the unquenchable spirit that neither the enemy nor the hurricane could ever defeat.

Slowly, without fuss, *Firefly* listed far down into the water, hesitated for a second and then capsized. A few more seconds and she was gone on the long road to the bottom. As the singing ceased abruptly, first one voice and then another in *Concord* took up the chorus in a last salute:

'Bless 'em all, bless 'em all,
The long and the short and the tall...'

There was a shout from the bridge and the men on deck looked up to see a figure standing in the damaged port wing waving his cap.

'Bless 'em all! God bless them!'

It was Strong, silhouetted against the grey, heavy sky. The safety valve had been forced open and for a brief moment the Captain had become an ordinary human being, inspired by the unflinching example of his comrades.

Masefield wiped an oily hand across his face as he let his glowing eyes rest on Strong. He grinned and murmured softly to himself, 'And bless you too.'

Firefly died on January 6, the twenty-sixth day of the hurricane, at 1528. Two minutes later *Concord* resumed her course for St John's, her wireless operators were sending the news to the Admiralty, and Strong had sent for Masefield and the Chief.

The First Lieutenant reported to the bridge first. Strong was back in his wooden seat, his face impassive.

'Number One, you did a good job. Thank you. I shall see their Lordships hear about it. How many men did you save?'

'Twenty, sir. All ratings.'

'All ratings. That's how it should be, Number One. I just can't imagine any of the leader's officers leaving him. He was one of the best-liked men in the Service.' Strong paused, his mind dwelling on the last scenes aboard *Firefly*. He came back to the present reluctantly. 'Try and get rid of some of that oil, John, and send for Sterling and the Mid to come up. I want to thank them myself.'

As Masefield turned away, Murray arrived and Strong took him into the chartroom to work out how far they could steam on the few remaining tons of oil. The bridge messenger found the Mid and then continued his search for Sterling. He hunted through the ship for a quarter of an hour before returning to the bridge to report with puzzlement that he could not find the Sub-Lieutenant.

The reason was being explained to the Captain by Prentice.

'Soon as we came alongside *Firefly,* sir, I saw Sub-Lieutenant Sterling jump on to her deck from the motor boat and start pushing men into the boat. I didn't see him for a couple of minutes while we were busy getting the motor boat packed tight. Then I looked again for a signal to bear away and I saw Sub-Lieutenant Sterling arguing with someone. He pushed a man into the motor boat and we began to pull away. He stayed behind, sir, aboard *Firefly*.'

9

A new danger threatened the battered *Concord* — ice. Temperatures skulked well below freezing point; spray and water froze before they ran off decks and superstructure. Long, flat, spiky icicles hung from the rigging and hard ice as much as a foot thick covered the sides of the bridge and the exposed gun positions. In Chief's estimate the extra weight increased her tonnage by a third.

She answered the helm sluggishly and lay even lower in the seas. Most frightening of all were the long, heavy rolls when the ice heeled her over and all that prevented the final topple was the ship's own buoyancy.

They were still 146 miles from St John's and once again more or less hove to, rolling, pitching and fighting to survive.

No illusions remained about their chances of reaching safety. The oil pumped overboard to assist *Firefly* had destroyed optimism, and it seemed that the hurricane could be relied upon to render impossible a transfer of fuel at sea from a rescue ship. It was also unlikely that a towrope could be secured on the ice-covered decks.

Even young Randall, now recovered from his hysterical outburst of fear, could recognize that once the oil tanks ran dry *Concord* must stop and wallow at the mercy of the storm. The sound of splitting seams and bulging bulkheads had become part of their lives, making the chief stoker the busiest man aboard. His working party maintained a non-stop guard against incoming water; as fast as one plate was shored up, another cracked.

The smell of sickness was everywhere. Toilets had been given up long ago, and those not usually affected by the roughest weather were revolted by their sloshing contents which leaked out into the mess decks. Bread and tinned food had vanished. From Strong to Randall, it was ship's biscuits and cocoa three times a day.

Only the bridge personnel kept watches — and these had been reduced to one hour at a time, the most a man could stand before freezing into lethargic uselessness.

At 0500 on January 7 a hush fell over the Atlantic. *Concord* burst through the tumult into an awful oasis of silence; the peace that comes before the last plunge. It seemed that they had earned some respite and a door had been slammed on the raging of the hurricane, the shrieking of the wind, shutting it out to enclose them in a soundproof cell of loneliness.

The crushing pressure of snow, ice, wind and rain vanished; the mighty blows of the sea calmed and the swell ran no higher or swifter than was normal for the place and the time of year. There were those whose eyes blazed again with quick hope — on the threshold of disaster they had been saved.

The hurricane, they thought, was over.

But to the more experienced it was but the prelude to a fate from which the mind recoiled. They sensed the muggy clamminess of death in the air and knew they had entered that deceptively smooth centre of the storm from which there was no escape. They were sealed off, and before their already slender hopes could be fulfilled they must break for freedom through the other side of the hurricane. In the lonesome hours that followed there were many who turned to God.

Strong and Masefield, undistinguishable beneath the layers of clothes and coats that kept some semblance of warmth close to their bodies, stood hunched near the wrecked port side of the bridge. Grant relieved Guns as Officer of the Watch and immediately revealed his inexperience by cheerfully admitting astonishment.

'I can hardly believe it,' he announced. 'I never thought storms died as quickly as this.'

Strong replied without moving. 'It's not over, Grant. We're moving through the centre of the depression. It will probably be worse than ever when we hit the other side — or rather, when it hits us.'

The weird quietness wore on, the men on *Concord*'s bridge staring wide-eyed and silent into the black night. Dawn came dully grey and, under Masefield's supervision, the forenoon was occupied by all hands cleaning out mess decks, shoring up damage and clearing away wreckage. The galley came alive and the crew were given their first hot meal in two weeks. Spirits rose, and a dogged will to survive swept through the ship.

From the bridge came a report that in answer to Strong's signal for help St John's and Argentia, the United States base in Newfoundland, were sending out assistance. With this knowledge to fortify them, the elements could strike again and they would be ready.

The hurricane returned to the attack at dusk. From afar came the low whimper of a turbulent, monstrous world. A new tension gripped the men, and suddenly the full fury of the hurricane tore at *Concord* with a howling and screaming that left men paralysed and numbed with awe.

The wind came with such ferocity and so dreadfully that it seemed the little destroyer must be blown into eternity. Above her, black-and-grey ghostly patches raced past like harbingers of evil while she tossed and rolled wildly, yawing in all directions.

It was a fearful, shocking glimpse into hell.

Breathing was difficult in a wind that forced the breath back into their throats, and eyes were tightly shut to ward off the impact of snow and hail.

The twenty-seventh day. How many more?

At 1500 Strong was in the chartroom at the back of the bridge when he felt a strange premonition of danger. He looked up and saw a green mountain of water filling the porthole. He made a dive for the doorway but was hurled back as the sea struck with such force that *Concord* trembled under the impact. Complete destruction was imminent; Strong could sense it in the violent vibrations running through the ship. Sheer weight of water was forcing her down under the sea as tons upon tons of it engulfed her, pouring in a noisy storm over the bridge, down passageways, wrecking everything it crossed. Bulkheads collapsed and steel scuttles sealing off portholes along the starboard side were crushed and scattered; in the forepart, the chain locker, paint shop and galley were reduced to twisted metal. Strong's cabin and all the officers' cabins were totally washed out and destroyed.

Strong made another rush to leave the chartroom and met head-on a sister wave which stove in the starboard side of the chartroom and flung him against the port bulkhead. He collapsed to the deck with a sobbing moan. The flood swamped over him, and when it drained away he was a pain-filled heap, unable to move in the sodden weight of his clothes.

He lay on the deck for several minutes before gathering his thoughts and willing himself to clamber to his feet, face twisted in the agony of effort. The water had thrown him against the large brass butterfly screw which bolted down the porthole scuttle. It had smashed down into the back of his neck to shatter his collarbone.

He stumbled out through an avalanche of sea to the wheelhouse and looked round at the chaos. Men lay where they had been thrown, bruised, bleeding and senseless. Only the bosun's mate and quartermaster reacted as Strong yelled his orders, obeying instinctively rather than knowingly.

Grant lay in a corner, eyes staring, but unmoving.

The passing moments were tense, fraught with thoughts that *Concord* had been given the final blow. The wheel spun from the quartermaster's hands, running free.

'Steering's broken down, sir,' he cried out.

Masefield emerged from the gloom and, with the bosun's mate at his heels, ran down to man the tiller flat — the emergency steering in the stern where the rudder quadrant could be moved manually.

Strong fought *Concord* back to face the hurricane with the main engines, using propellers to keep her nose on course while the emergency steering was being organized. He estimated the damage. *Concord* had come out of the buffeting bloody but still unbeaten. The starboard side had been ripped to pieces, whole chunks of metal torn away. Only the motor boat on the port side remained; even a machine-gun mounting had been ripped out and thrown overboard.

Minutes later, the First Lieutenant returned to report the tiller flat manned and the emergency steering working with Guns in charge.

'Time we got out of here, Number One.' It was a slight catch in Strong's voice that made Masefield start.

'Are you hurt, sir?'

'Nothing serious, Number One. Doc can have a look at it later. First, this is not the place for us. I'm going to turn round and run before the storm. Better warn everyone.'

Masefield paled. To try turning a ship in this sea would be more certain suicide than holding a revolver to one's own head and pulling the trigger. He was about to speak when Strong grasped his arm.

'Don't stand there and argue, Number One. For God's sake, get busy. Signalman, man the telephone to the tiller flat.'

Masefield left the bridge, smarting at the Captain's unexpected anger. He had not yet absorbed the extent to which *Concord* was suffering and, unlike Strong, had not realized that the ship would never survive another blow like the last two.

Strong watched the restless sea for an opportunity. A long series of moving, white-grey dunes stretched out ahead. This was the moment.

'Signalman — hard a-starboard.'

The order was shouted over the telephone, and in the tiller flat six men pulled at the emergency wheel operated without mechanical aid. It was their strength against the power of the sea. Slowly and in spasmodic jerks the wheel forced the rudder round and *Concord* began to turn.

The men on the bridge who had recovered gripped railings and stanchions for support and watched, fascinated by the awful slowness of the turn. It was a daring manoeuvre in those mountainous seas, any one of which might catch them beam on and flick *Concord* right over.

Then she began to turn faster as though she too had caught the urgency of the moment and, frantic for her safety, was hurrying to run away from the tempest. She came round without incident and, with wind and sea no longer in her face but now beating down on her starboard quarter, she ran away; heading anywhere as long as it would give her a chance to outlive the hurricane. Only a day and a half from refuge, she had been forced to retreat further into the raging Atlantic, cruelly exposed to the icy blasts of the never-ending wind and sea.

Strong spoke to Murray in the engine room. 'How much longer can we keep up steam, Chief?'

'About thirty hours. I've been using only one boiler for the last couple of days.'

Strong felt suddenly elated. 'Good man. That's ten hours more than I thought. We're running before the storm now, but that shouldn't be necessary for longer than four or five hours. If St John's sent a tug out this morning, we might rendezvous by tomorrow morning. Keep it up, Chief.'

He put down the telephone and even the pain in his back seemed to ease at the excitement of new hope.

'Messenger, tell the doctor to come up, please.'

By 1800 Strong was searching the seas with narrowed eyes. It seemed improbable, but for the first time his ears had detected a different note in the noise of the storm. It was less fierce, less erratic, more steady. The treatment to his shoulder, the support of the arm sling and the effect of drugs had shredded the tiredness away and he was alert for any change that would enable him to bring *Concord* round and point her once more, to head this time in the general direction of St John's.

For thirty minutes there had been no dangerous seas, and his growing conviction that the hurricane had passed its peak was confirmed when Boland came on watch and said, 'Seems to have died away a bit, sir. Still rough, but that blasted wind isn't so strong, I'm sure.'

'You're right, Pilot. We'll turn back. Warn the engine room and mess decks. Signalman — tell the tiller flat — hard a-starboard.'

Again they turned without incident and the pummelling from the head-on sea began once more, lacking however the ferocious power that had caused so much damage. Insistent, uncomfortable, and still threatening, it nevertheless allowed them the right to proceed at nearly ten knots.

'Thank heavens we got through the worst part on the other side of the depression, sir,' said Boland as they stood unprotected amid the confusion of the bridge.

'Yes. And we can thank the people who built this ship, whoever they were. Boston firm, I think. Somewhere around 1918. That reminds me, Pilot. When we get in, I want a copy of our log book and Report of Proceedings sent to them. No ship is built to float in what we've been through, and they might like to know just what their workmanship can really stand.'

Boland smiled in the darkness. Just like the Old Man to think of a thing like that and deliberately use the word 'when' and not 'if'. It might be the last of the hurricane, but it was still strong enough to sink them if they ran out of fuel.

The engine-room telephone buzzer interrupted his thoughts; it heralded news of another tragedy. The chief stoker, who for days had been working tirelessly to control damage and leaks, had not been seen in the engine room for two hours. Search parties had combed the ship without finding him.

It was a dreadful shock to Strong. He questioned Murray, and the picture emerged that the great-hearted stoker, though warned to keep off the upper deck, must have discovered some new and dangerous damage needing immediate attention. His loyalty to his ship and shipmates had probably cost him his life.

Some time during the day he had been picked up by a victim-seeking wave and carried overboard. In the howling hell and unholy commotion of the hurricane no human shout or scream for help could possibly have been heard.

Rear-Admiral Charles Quigley stood in the Convoy Operations Room at his headquarters in St John's. Two staff officers flanked him, and six Wrens moved quietly and efficiently about the large map of the western Atlantic, plotting movements of ships, aircraft and U-boats.

Admiral Quigley, fair but nearly grey, dapper but not immaculate, and short without being small, spoke in a quiet crisp accent inherited from the plains of western Canada.

'*Whirlpool* is in *Concord*'s area. Signal her to search for *Concord* and stand by to assist. The tug *Mormon* should reach her vicinity by noon tomorrow. Let's hope the weather will ease enough to get a tow across.'

'*Concord*'s going to have a rough time if she runs out of fuel in this lot, sir,' said the senior staff officer.

'You're right, but, by God, Louis Strong's brought her through plenty. He won't give up too easily. What's the overall position of that convoy?'

'Four merchant ships unaccounted for so far, sir. And of the escort, *Firefly*, *Vine* and *Campdown* lost. Rest have all reported in and seem to have come through, all seriously damaged. Only *Concord* is uncertain. And, frankly, I don't give much for her chances.'

'You're an incorrigible pessimist.'

'No, sir. But even if *Whirlpool* does find her, what can she do? And the odds are against *Mormon* doing much more.'

The Admiral gave his staff officers a sardonic look. Then he grinned. 'Tell you what. I'll bet you the best dinner you've had on this station that Strong brings his ship in on the end of a tow or under his own steam.'

The two officers glanced at each other.

'That's a bet, sir. And one we just don't want to win.'

That night, ice enclosed the limping *Concord.* She burrowed through the seas shrouded in a ghostly gleam of white. On the bridge, officers and men were wedged at their stations, coats, caps and faces glistening with tiny particles of frost. Not long after 2200, the starboard quarter lookout blinked to clear his frozen eyelids. He thought there had been a dark shape coming up from astern, but the blur was indistinguishable in the fine, driving snow.

He searched the area again, sweeping slowly from dead astern out to the starboard beam. A light winked at him and in sheer astonishment he jumped backwards and shouted excitedly, 'Ship bearing abaft starboard beam, sir. Green 140.'

Boland was pulled back to the present, his thoughts of himself and *Concord* during the past days swept aside by the urgency of the present. The signalman joined him on the side of the bridge.

'Giving the challenge, sir.'

'Right, reply then.' Boland felt relief surge through him. For days and nights he had lived with a private dread — that the war might have caught up with him, not through the enemy but in the shape of the hurricane. His future, so assured in the days when they had left Liverpool, had begun to fade with every new assault from the sea. He had not revealed his convictions, but they had crystallized with each series of emergencies. His once so neatly pigeonholed personal plan had become a rather dreary, egotistical, even pompous pipe dream. And more surprising, he had been able to recognize it as such. Peter Boland had changed — but he gave no sign of it, nor would he admit it fully to himself, yet.

The signalman's voice reached him. 'It's the *Whirlpool,* sir.'

'Tell the Captain, will you?'

'Aye, aye, sir.'

Strong had slept amid the wreckage of the wardroom for four hours, a deep undisturbed sleep, carefully protected by a barrier erected by the deliberate refusal of officers and men to work near him. For that reason the cabin flat was cleared up, leaving untouched only the wardroom where the Captain slept on, too tired even to snore.

He clambered to the bridge, sleep clinging stubbornly to his eyes, but his erect carriage reflecting the benefit of the rest. *Whirlpool* was closer and her silhouette clearly definable. She had exchanged challenge and reply before daring to use R/T. Now her Captain called *Concord* and asked for Strong. He was a half-stripe, and four years junior to Strong.

'What can we do, sir?'

'Got any spare fuel?'

'Yes, but we'll never be able to transfer it in this weather.'

'No, but if you stay in company it might ease off by tomorrow. Where's *Mormon*?'

'Can't say, sir. She's heading out to meet you after dawn. The Yanks have sent their big tug, *Searay*, from Argentia. She'll probably make a rendezvous about noon.'

'Good. Well, nice of you to come, we could do with company. Keep station four cables on my starboard beam.'

But the hurricane had not yet finished with them. After midnight the seas rose in a final, furious attack on the victim who might yet cheat them of victory. The snow fell thickly, blotting out even the bows, and again *Concord* hove to.

At dawn *Whirlpool* had vanished; attempts to call her on R/T brought no reply. She had given confidence to the desperate men aboard *Concord* by her presence; alone once more, they were reduced to an even lower state of despair than before. Chief set the seal on their plight. He reported to Strong, 'Fuel tanks about empty, sir. I'm sending men down into them to bale out the dregs.'

They were still eighty miles from St John's, making five knots. On the bridge, eyes searched anxiously for *Mormon* while Masefield muttered testily, 'She's got radar; surely she can't miss us.'

For the next few hours stokers and seamen climbed down into the thick slime and cloying fumes of the fuel tanks to scrape clean the bottoms and walls with every available tin. Hands and feet slipped in the precious dregs, but the work went on doggedly — each tin of salvaged oil could give life. A human chain passed the tins to the diesel burners, which consumed the contents as fast as it was passed through the feed valves.

At noon *Concord* was still steaming, her engines kept alive by the sliding and the scraping, the cursing and the scooping of the men in the fuel tanks. Chief rang the bridge to speak to the Captain.

'Running on prayers now, sir. That extra effort this morning dried us out.'

Strong, to the astonishment of the men around him, gave a cheerful laugh. 'Not to worry, Chief. *Mormon* will get here soon; perhaps the American tug *Searay*. Keep on praying.'

'I know only one prayer, sir, and even God must be getting bored with it. Wonder if He answers sinners? Incidentally, I've got someone down in the tanks doing yeoman work.'

'Who's that?'

'Doc. He's been down in the for'ard fuel tank for the last hour.'

'Get him out, Chief. He will gas himself, and we've too many injured that need his care. Tell him thanks from me.'

While *Concord* stumbled on and the expected arrival of the two tugs occupied all thoughts, Strong called Masefield to discuss the sort of nagging worry that is never far from a commander's mind when at sea and at war — the behaviour of his officers.

'About Grant, Number One. What do you think?'

Masefield sighed gloomily as though finally trapped by some obscure but persistent duty. 'Well, I'm afraid I was expecting this, sir. And trying to avoid it. He's been frightened a couple of times. When we went over to *Firefly* —'

Strong interjected, 'Yes, I know about that. There was another time up here when one heavy sea broke over us and he literally cowered in a corner. Not good enough.'

There was a brief silence before Masefield replied. 'Still, it is his first real trip, sir. He might steady up a bit after a little more experience.'

'Can't wait for that, Number One. He's not built for the sea, though of all of us he is probably the best-looking physical specimen. Funny, but in spite of his frailty, young Sterling had double his guts. Shows how wrong we can be. I put down Sterling as the one who might have panicked.'

Masefield looked ahead woodenly.

'No,' continued Strong. 'I'll have to recommend him for shore duty after this. Bloody unpleasant business,' he ended in exasperation. Masefield still didn't reply and Strong glanced at him curiously. 'How's that feud of yours with Boland progressing? Come to a full stop, I hope.'

The First Lieutenant stiffened. 'No feud, sir. There hasn't been much time in the last few days. He has done his share of the work and behaved himself below.'

The Captain relaxed. 'He is another paradox. Bloody-minded as hell one minute, but pretty efficient once the chips are down. Don't underestimate his qualities, John.'

Boland himself came from the chartroom to stand with them and automatically lifted his binoculars for a search to port. He had just begun the sweep when he stopped, peered intently and shouted, 'Ship bearing red twenty, sir. It's a tug, I think.'

Glasses swung round and a signal lamp flashed from the new arrival. The Yeoman answered the challenge and called out, 'It's *Searay,* sir. Says: "Want a drink or a tow?"'

Strong grinned. 'Reply: "Many thanks for coming. Try a tow, please, it's too cold for milkshakes."'

As soon as the signal had been passed, the sturdy little tug swung round to take position ahead of *Concord* while the destroyer's crew lined the decks, sending cheer after cheer across the decreasing noise of the flagging storm.

Boland looked at Masefield steadily. 'Well, John, looks like we are going to make it after all.' It was said without malice, without hidden meaning. Yet the First Lieutenant reacted as if stung.

'Shut up, Boland. I might not want her any more, but I'll make bloody sure you don't have her.'

Misery flooded his eyes. He was sure Boland had alluded to the leave they would all get after this trip. But the Navigator was looking at him dejectedly, almost sadly.

Strong overheard Masefield's rejoinder and intervened furiously. 'My God, you two will answer to me for this stupid pettiness when we reach harbour.' Having heard the First Lieutenant only, he had also quite wrongly assumed that Boland had returned to the attack. 'Get off this bridge, Mister Boland, and take charge of the towing party on the foredeck.'

But Masefield had swung round angrily to the top of the ladder. 'I'll do it, sir,' he said, and vanished below.

Boland said quietly to the silent Strong, 'Honestly, sir, I was being perfectly friendly.'

'Oh, for heaven's sake, shut up.'

Resentment, anger and the awful sick feeling that always came when he thought of Sonia mingled in Masefield as he followed the ten men of the towing party out to the foredeck. They slithered on the pitching, icy plates and made their way for'ard in sudden spurts from one support to the next. The First Lieutenant reached the fo'c'sle and hung on grimly to a guard rail as *Searay* dropped down close.

Thirty feet separated the stem of the destroyer and the stern of the tug, a dangerous manoeuvre, and after admiring the cool judgment of the American skipper he raised a hand and a seaman hurled a throwing line across the gap. For a moment the line was caught by the wind and looked as if it might fall into the sea, but one of the tug crew leapt to the gunwale, caught it and fell back to safety.

Quickly the line was made fast to a heavy towrope and the men on *Concord*'s fo'c'sle began hauling it in across the narrow gap of stormy seas. The capstan could not be used as the slight steam available was needed for the engines.

The hauling stopped temporarily as *Concord*'s bows rose over a large wave, but resumed as they fell down the other side. A startled cry from the bridge was carried away in the wind, but Masefield had seen the danger. Another wave was racing down on them with unexpected speed, threatening to engulf the fo'c'sle.

'Hold on to something!' he yelled, and leapt across to wrap his arms round the port anchor chain.

In the next second tons of water crashed down upon *Concord* and the foredeck disappeared in a turmoil of raging sea. Masefield felt a body bump against him and let go his grip on the anchor chain to grab at it. Instead, he was washed over the deck as well, scrabbling with desperate fingers to find a hold.

He felt something hit his head and reached up to grasp it with both hands — a wire, a guard-rail wire. He must be near the ship's side. Frantically he locked his arms round the wire and felt his legs and body slip over the side, to leave him hanging by his arms. The ship rose again, and as the water washed away sudden panic swept over him — he was over the side with two of the working party, who were also gripping the guard rail.

On the bridge Strong and Boland gazed down at the foredeck in stunned horror. Two more men were struggling to regain their feet in an attempt to help Masefield and their two shipmates. But *Concord*'s bows came down with another crash, and again the foredeck was covered with boiling, surging water.

It seemed to the watchers on the bridge that an eternity passed before she rose clear and the seas ran down and away. And when the deck came clear only six figures in oilskins ran stumblingly back to safety. Of Masefield there was no sign.

Boland, rigid and paralysed by the sudden disaster which had come on the threshold of rescue, recoiled inside himself at a tiny whisper in his stricken mind. If the First Lieutenant had not been so angry and stormed down to the foredeck in such haste, it might have been him.

The thought blossomed and filled his mind. He glanced guiltily at Strong, but the Captain was still staring, outwardly impassive, at the guard rail to which Masefield had clung in his last moments of life. In that sea there could be no hope of picking up the lost five; even their lifebelts would be useless.

The tug, which had been thrown down on *Concord* and had nearly hit her, had drawn over to starboard and a light blinked from her bridge.

'*Searay,* sir,' cried the Yeoman. '"Sorry, still too bad to try towing. Will stand by you."'

Strong nodded automatically, his sailor's mind registering the correctness of the American tug's decision while his private thoughts raced in a confused mixture of misery, sorrow and anger at the loss of his First Lieutenant and the man who had come nearest to being his friend.

With startling illogic, he swung round on Boland. His voice was little more than a whisper, but it lashed the Navigator with the force of a whip thong. 'Now perhaps you are happy, Mister Boland. You hated him, goaded him and made his life hell. If it hadn't been for you, he would never have been there, he would be alive now. You should have been the one, not he.'

The Navigator stared wide-eyed at his Captain's white, drawn face. Then with an inarticulate mumble he ran from the bridge, away from the blazing hatred that lay in Strong's moist eyes.

The engine-room telephone rang. Strong answered it. 'Yes, what is it?'

'Chief here, sir. We've scraped the bottom of the barrel. Not even prayers will help now.'

'Can we use wood or something?'

'Yes, we could keep a little steam up with plenty of wood, or anything burnable.'

'Right, we'll start breaking up every bit of wood in the ship.' Strong slammed down the receiver, shook himself in an effort to clear his mind, and turned to the bosun's mate. 'Tell the First Lieutenant I want him here right away.'

The bosun's mate looked blank. The First Lieutenant had been washed overboard. Who did the Captain mean? Then realization dawned slowly. Lieutenant Boland was now acting Number One.

10

Under Boland's orders, the crew set about stripping the ship of everything burnable. First to suffer were the officers' cabins, from which wardrobes, toilet cupboards, chests of drawers, even bunks were broken up and sent down to the engine room.

The wardroom was next; chairs, tables, sideboards and lockers joining the growing mound of chopped wood on the side of the engine-room hatch.

The Petty Officers' accommodation followed and, last to be attacked, the seamen's and stokers' messes produced a wealth of locker wood liberally sprinkled with gorgeous pin-up pictures. Steam was maintained on one boiler only, and *Concord* drifted over the dying storm at five knots, with *Searay* in constant attendance to starboard. There was still no sign of the lost *Whirlpool* or the errant tug *Mormon.*

Strong kept his vigil on the bridge, determined not to submit to the clawing, jagged edges of weariness until his ship was safe. He signalled St John's: 'Fuel tanks scraped dry. Weather impossible for towing. Am steaming on furniture. Regret cannot estimate ETA. *Searay* standing by.'

When this message was received at headquarters, Admiral Quigley passed it across to his staff officers with a confident chuckle.

'Looks like I might yet win that dinner from you chaps,' he said, rubbing his considerable stomach in anticipation. His appetite was renowned, his capacity for good wines unrivalled. The officers groaned good-humouredly. Like Quigley, they were watching *Concord*'s progress with increasing admiration for the skill of her captain and the endurance of her crew.

On board the destroyer, a strange tension had taken a firm hold on the survivors. The hurricane was blowing itself out and, by nightfall, they might take *Searay*'s towline. But rumours of the Captain's outburst with the Navigator had spread and curious glances followed Boland as he walked in Masefield's shoes, organizing the break-up of the ship's equipment. The acting First Lieutenant was being ruthlessly efficient about this — the chartroom table with its cumbersome wooden structure for holding charts was ripped out and subjected to the axe; the Captain's desk and furniture followed suit; even the small table from the wireless room was sacrificed. Wooden cupboards were found in the wheelhouse, and the flag locker aft of the bridge helped feed the hungry boiler.

Strong cursed himself silently. No matter what his personal convictions, his attack on Boland on the bridge of his ship had been unforgivable. He knew he should apologize but his stubborn nature locked the words in his throat. Instead, he treated Boland formally, receiving politeness in return.

If the rest of the officers felt strongly one way or the other about Masefield's loss, they gave no indication of their thoughts. Chief remained on permanent duty in the engine room; Doc tended the sick and the wounded; Grant, Guns and the Mid took their turns on watch, staying out of the way and avoiding both Strong and Boland as much as possible. The only apparent difference was that Harry Prentice found the problem of how to address Boland solved for him. Automatically, he transferred to him the 'sir' he gave to all First Lieutenants.

Bill Gridley expressed the views of the lower deck as he splintered his own mess-deck table with an axe. 'What the ruddy 'ell is it to us if the officers don't like each other? They got their troubles like we got ours. This lot'll need a refit when we get into 'arbour and the chances are we'll all be on draft for a new ship in a coupla days. It ain't none of our business, I'm tellin' yer.' He glowered across at O'Flynn. 'And I got news for you, matey. I'm gonna wangle the kid into my draft, wherever that might be, see?'

The Irishman grinned back. 'That's all right, me boyo. The kid's got dough for the both of us. We'll see 'e comes with us and we'll share the loot when this bloody lot's over, eh?'

Gridley nodded craftily. It suited him to let O'Flynn think an agreement had been reached. Meanwhile, young Randall's future on the lower decks was assured, for he had unwittingly acquired two fervent protectors, and Gridley would find some way of double-crossing O'Flynn before long. The day Germany surrendered would be the day he would break this truce.

He wiped a brittle, cold hand on his shirt and proffered it to O'Flynn.

At three o'clock that afternoon the rain stopped and the mist lifted. For the first time in three weeks the open seas spread out around them. Despite the ice, the wetness, the discomfort, the lack of proper food and the miserable conditions throughout the ship, it was possible to feel the lightening of hearts, the resurgence of spirit, the draining of tension.

Boland reported to Strong, 'We are nearly down to rock bottom on wood, sir. What about clothes and some sorts of food?'

'Why not? See the Chief and find out what else will burn for him.'

As Boland left, Strong saw how much the man had changed. The affected, supercilious twist of the mouth had been replaced by tight, compressed lips pulling tautly at the skin of his face, thinning it down and revealing an unexpected hardness of chin and bone; the lazy, indolent body had toughened, grown leaner and more erect. *A thousand pities,* he thought, *that Peter Boland should have made his mistakes and become a man in my ship.*

An almost hysterical shout interrupted his thoughts. 'Land on the port beam, sir.' The word raced round the ship and men rushed to the guard rail to see the faint bruise on the horizon.

'St John's!' shouted Gridley.

Boland returned to the bridge and consulted his charts with Strong. Signals were exchanged with *Searay* to confirm their position, and in reply to a query from the American as to whether *Concord* was ready for a tow, Strong replied, 'Don't you dare touch me. We will make it under our own steam if it costs us our clothes.'

'Suggest that might be a bit drastic in this weather,' *Searay* signalled back. 'We will keep our hands off you while you undress.'

In effect, *Concord* was being denuded. Chief mixed the wood with broken-up leather armchairs, certain types of food and old clothes — anything that would keep the fires burning. The engine room itself was stripped down by the greedy stokers who struggled to keep *Concord* steaming at her five knots.

When only three miles from harbour, Strong felt confident enough to signal: 'My ETA 1630. Engine-room cannibals have devoured everything but the galley stove.'

And shortly after 4 p.m. *Concord* passed the marker buoy at the channel entrance to move slowly, listing under the ice, into sheltered waters. The port signal station called up to flash: 'From Rear-Admiral St John's to *Concord.* Well done and welcome home.'

Covered in ice, her crew at stations for entering harbour looking bedraggled, bearded and dirty, and the mound of messy wood, food and clothing that fed the fires below reduced to a few scraps, the destroyer moved towards her berth.

She was still a hundred yards away when the propellers began to idle. Chief rang through to the bridge. 'That's it, sir. She's packed up for good now.'

Strong had brought *Concord* to safety with skill and luck playing their necessary role; yet there had been an even more powerful influence dominating himself and, through him, the fate of them all — faith. His uncompromising faith in their ship, in the determination of the crew to survive and in his own ability to lick the storm had given him the strength to endure the worst without flagging and had controlled the fits of depression and moods of black despair that somehow had been hidden. Throughout it all his grim, set face had revealed none of the fears that had beset him almost daily. Instead, he had shown a stubborn, confident front which would not admit defeat; would show only a constant faith.

Even at this moment of idle propellers within sight of the berth, he was reluctant to accept assistance which might tarnish the triumph that was their rightful reward.

Searay lay off, ready to answer any call for help. In her tiny wheelhouse the young American Lieutenant in command gazed along the length of *Concord* and said to his junior officer, 'Take a good look at that ship. Now she's steady you can see what she's been through. Foredeck smashed about, bridge wrecked, boats and davits gone, gun mountings ripped to shreds, depth charges gone. Holy cow, I'd hate to see what's happened inside her. Now what's happened? She's stopped.'

His eyes swung to the propeller wake. 'Good God, her screws have packed up. Hand me that loudhailer mike.'

He paused with the microphone in his hand. 'No,' he muttered almost to himself, 'that's the sort of skipper who won't use any tow from me if he can help it. He's got to make it, somehow. It's only a few lousy yards.'

He lifted the mike.

Strong was still searching for a solution to his idle engines when the American's voice cut through the cold evening air.

'Hey, Captain. Congratulations; you made harbour. Tell you what, I'll just nudge you in. Won't count as help.'

Strong's frosty lips cracked in a slight grin. But he was reluctant to accept even this token assistance. The young American read his thoughts.

'Come on, Captain. A little cheat now won't hurt anyone.'

At a sudden wave from Strong, the tug's nose brushed against *Concord*'s battered starboard side in what was almost a gentle, tender caress, yet hard enough to push her slowly towards the jetty. Heaving lines spanned the water gap, followed by mooring ropes and wires. A small group of dockyard workers moved across the quay towards the ship, gesticulating among themselves as they pointed out the storm damage. Then they raised a slight cheer. There was no response from the tired, listless crew. They had neither the strength nor the inclination to celebrate — they merely wanted sleep and warmth, and more warmth.

Strong forced himself to give the shadow of a smile to Boland. 'We've made it, Number One. Let's give Chief a shock. Ring down "finished with engines".'

Boland tugged at the engine-room telegraph and stared hard at his Captain. Strong was patting the front of the bridge and, although his lips were closed, Boland could imagine him putting the gallant little ship to bed. Like a husband who has been forced to bring his wife through the worst experiences of hardship in their lives, he was soothing the torture from her tired, aching body; safe and secure at last, she could relax until specialists came to heal the wounds.

On the foredeck O'Flynn tapped the coxswain on the shoulder. 'Hey, Cox, what about letting us grab some of that wood ashore to start some fires going? Even St Mary herself would freeze in this begotten land.'

As he finished speaking, Boland came down from the bridge. At the coxswain's enquiry he nodded his agreement.

'And, O'Flynn, see there's enough for an officers' fire as well.'

'Aye, aye, sir.' The Leading Seaman shouted to his mates and hands followed him across the rail on to the jetty, eagerly scavenging for wood.

Two immaculate, well-fed-looking officers strode through the crowd of sailors to the gangway — a Commander and Lieutenant from base headquarters. The former remarked caustically on the lack of respect being shown by 'this bunch of hooligans. Why, they are all dressed alike, in rags. Can't tell one from the other?

Mid spotted the strangers approaching the gangway and, shouting to the bosun's mate, he ran to greet them. The bosun's mate could hardly hold the tiny whistle in his thickly mittened hands, but he managed a reedy pipe as the Mid stood to attention, saluting.

To the Commander's astonishment there was nothing to distinguish the bedraggled figures greeting him as an officer and a rating. They looked almost alike; doubles, in fact, of the crowd gathering wood ashore.

By now, bonfires were bursting into flame along the upper deck, each with its complement of hooded, duffel-coated men huddled around it basking in the warm glow. The Commander enquired for Strong and Mid pointed to a weird, unique group clad in assorted clothing, sharing a slightly larger fire than the rest.

It was Strong, Grant, Guns, Boland and Chief. Their faces, set in cold, frosty lines with tiny icicles glistening from their hair and eyelashes, gave no sign of welcome.

The visitors coughed hesitantly and the Commander asked pompously, 'Lieutenant-Commander Strong?'

Strong lifted his head and nodded slightly. The Commander frowned at the lack of formality. But there was something about *Concord*'s Captain that warned him not to press the point too far. Strong reflected all that the destroyer and her men had suffered. His face was burned darkly red by the raw, icy wind; his eyes were mere gleaming specks, forced back into their sockets by lack of sleep; his body was rigidly tensed, still being forced to stay upright by the indomitable will-power that had refused to be defeated by the hurricane.

The Commander plunged towards disaster. 'Are these your officers? Surely they could wear caps or something to show their ranks?'

Strong gazed down at the fire. His voice was without emotion.

'We're not dressed for harbour yet. And until we get thawed out a bit, not even the Admiral could get a salute from these boys.'

The Commander's eyes took in their oilskins, duffel coats, drenched mufflers and sweaters.

'We will talk about that later. I have orders for you to accompany us back to headquarters. The Admiral wants to see you.'

Strong's eyes glinted with a flicker of sudden anger.

'Oh, for heaven's sake, sir, can't you see I'm in no shape to see anyone, not even the Admiral? Give me a chance to warm up, then I'll find some sort of uniform and call on him. If you want to help, make arrangements for my crew to be put up ashore somewhere warm. They can't spend another night aboard this ship.'

'The Admiral won't like being kept waiting.'

'I'll remember that. Now suppose you make those arrangements.'

The Commander stiffened perceptibly. He had not expected to be treated so diffidently, neither had he planned to stand for so long in the cold. 'I'll pass your request to the Chief Staff Officer. A car will call for you in fifteen minutes.' He turned away and, followed by the Lieutenant, stalked ashore.

Fifteen minutes passed silently while officers and men hunched over their fires, too tired to talk, content to soak up the meagre warmth.

Two cars drew up on the jetty and the sound of slamming doors reached the upper deck without awakening apparent interest. Doc Goodwin and the Mid had joined the group at the officers' fire, and all seven were startled to hear a brusque voice say loudly, 'Which one of you heathens is the captain of this ship?'

Mid looked up first, and his subsequent struggle to clamber to his feet told Strong that he had better make an effort to see who had arrived. His head twisted slowly, gazed for a moment at the large, portly figure in the greatcoat, wearing an Admiral's epaulettes, and then he too was hurrying with the rest to climb to attention.

'I am, sir. Lieutenant-Commander Strong.'

Quigley looked down at him cheerfully.

'My God, Strong, it's good to see you. Couldn't recognize you in that rig. You had us worried for a few days, you know.'

'Sorry, sir. I intended reporting to you just as soon as I was warm enough to put some decent clothes on — that is, if I've got any left.'

'Don't bother. You and your officers are coming back with me in the cars. My staff will see to it that your chaps are looked after in the wardroom ashore and you can warm up while you tell me all about it.'

Strong looked past the Admiral, smiled at one of the staff officers he knew slightly, and went grim again as he recognized one of the previous callers, the Commander.

'Thank you, sir,' he said quietly. 'But I can't leave the ship until suitable arrangements have been made for the crew. I asked the Commander over there to look into it. I'd like to know what can be done.'

'All been attended to, Strong,' replied Quigley. 'Here are the buses coming now. Tell your chaps to get aboard and they will be taken to barracks straight away.'

At Strong's quick nod, Boland about-turned and left to organize the transfer of the crew ashore. Strong felt that it was time to make amends for not greeting the Admiral.

'I'm sorry there was no one to pipe you aboard, sir, but'

Quigley laughed away the explanation. 'Forget it. This is not the time for ceremony, even if some of my desk-riders seem to think so.' He glanced over his shoulder at the discomfited Commander.

Strong realized that he had been reported and was grateful to Quigley for ignoring the matter. *How typical of the Navy,* he thought wryly, *to bring a ship through the worst blasted hurricane in centuries and then expect the crew to be spick-and-span on arrival.* For a moment he experienced a twinge of regret that *Concord* had reached harbour. With the weather clearing, he would like to be back at sea again, far away from pompous protocol and constricting formalities.

They waited while the crew filed ashore, shepherded by Petty Officers. Boland hurried up to report that the shore patrol had mounted guard on *Concord* and, at Quigley's gesture, they followed him to the two waiting cars.

Doc, Chief, Boland, Grant, Guns and the Mid scrambled into the second car, with Grant complaining bitterly that the jetty moved almost as much as the ship. Mid said scornfully, 'Haven't you ever heard of the sailor's roll? The first few hours ashore you always roll a bit because the body is accustomed to the movement of the ship. Why, you haven't been at sea for a dog watch yet.'

'Now then, Mid,' chuckled Doc. 'Just because we are ashore again is no excuse to become your old objectionable self. Why, we found time to like you a bit on that trip.'

Prentice smiled at some secret joke. His eyes strayed to the passing dimmed lights. 'I have a mind to complete my education before we leave here. Acquire some insurance against having women thrown up in my face again.'

'You had better let an old hand give you some advice before you go looking for girls, young feller,' murmured Chief.

Boland laughed. 'That, Mid, is a dirty old man's way of saying he'd like to go along with you.'

The car stopped while the driver showed a pass to a sentry and then moved on smoothly to the base wardroom. This was really an extension of the Admiral's house, which in turn was an annexe to the officer's living quarters.

Later, in the Admiral's study, Strong savoured the first drink he had tasted since leaving Liverpool — a large whisky-and-water. Spare clothes had been produced and he stood in front of the electric fire dressed in grey flannel trousers, clean shirt, white scarf and uniform jacket — it belonged to another Lieutenant-Commander.

While they waited for dinner, Quigley sat in a large leather armchair listening to him describe the events of the last four weeks. He interrupted only to tell the young Canadian of circumstances he could know nothing about. By the time the Admiral's steward announced dinner, Strong had finished his story and his third whisky. Stiffness and aches were setting in as his body thawed, and the warm air of security swamped his mind like a relaxing drug.

Throughout dinner he talked, and knew he was talking too much. But the long days and nights of command when he could confide in no one, when he had to maintain, even at the most alarming times, an attitude of aloof detachment, had left behind them an uncontrollable urge to talk. Here was a senior officer who not only wanted him to speak but was prepared to listen. He talked.

With the coffee came brandy, and it was enough. His eyelids drooped, his body sagged and his mouth felt dry and dusty from too much talking. With muttered apologies, he said goodnight and stumbled down the long corridors to his room, where the whiteness of the turned-back sheets dazzled his eyes, now heavy with the pain of resisted sleep.

Whisky, unaccustomed food, sheer fatigue, warmth and, above all, the clean sheets played havoc with his mind. Without attempting to undress, he lay down on the bed as though it was his bunk in *Concord* and said quite clearly, 'Thank you, Number One.'

He was speaking to John Masefield.

The next morning dockyard workers and a holding crew took over *Concord* while her officers and ship's company moved into temporary quarters ashore pending a decision on the destroyer's future.

A large sack of mail from England and Ottawa had been waiting for them and, while Strong and Chief accompanied engineers from the Admiral's staff and the dockyard superintendent on an inspection of the ship's damage, Boland and Grant dealt with the official business.

In the evening Strong found a neat stack of unopened official and private letters for his personal attention. His mother persisted in using French in her own home and in correspondence. Long ago, it seemed now, this habit had lost its meaning for him. The Navy had removed him from the influence of family and Montreal, indoctrinated him with the clipped, stilted, formal language of the wardroom, impregnated him with a horror for Latin exaggeration and gesticulation, and imbued him with a correct affection for the classical British understatement.

He tossed the personal letters to one side of the table and turned to the official mail — requests for this, demands for that, why had he failed .... On it went, the formal business of commanding a ship, the practical application of brave, high principles to a vast complex organization of experts now swamped by amateurs. Fortunately the amateurs had invaded even the sanctums of administrators and routine was usually fouled up from the top downwards.

One envelope looked different from the rest — more important somehow with a red 'Confidential' stamped beside the Admiralty crest. He tore it open and pulled out a long formal letter attached to a press cutting. Intrigued, he read the letter first.

Sir — I am directed by Their Lordships of Admiralty to draw your attention to the attached cutting of an article which appeared in the Daily Bulletin of December 8, 1942.

(2) The contents are considered to be (a) a breach of the King's Regulations and Admiralty Instructions which forbid Naval officers to contribute to the Press without permission; (b) damaging to discipline and morale at sea and at home; (c) of considerable propaganda value to the enemy.

(3) Enquiries suggest that the 'Special Correspondent' might be one of your officers, Lieutenant P. Boland, R.N. V.R. You are instructed to question Lieutenant Boland on this matter in the presence of two reliable witnesses.

(4) Should Lieutenant Boland admit his authorship of the article he is to be placed under close arrest and charged with:

Conduct prejudicial to the discipline of the Service; conduct unbecoming to an Officer by rendering aid to the enemy in time of war.

(5) In this event, Rear-Admiral St John's will convene a disciplinary court at the first available opportunity to deal with these charges.

(6) Copies of all reports and statements are to be forwarded to the Secretary to the Board of Admiralty.

Strong read the letter a second time, his dazed mind unable to grasp the implications of Boland's actions. *Surely,* he thought, *this is a trivial matter.* He recalled rumours from the wardroom that Boland had been the author of several articles appearing in the *Bulletin.* They had been considered pretty good, even factual, at the time.

Feeling thoroughly at a loss, he tossed aside the letter and turned to the article. It was headed *Impostors in Uniform.*

The Battle of the Atlantic is real only to a minority of the officers in certain Commands. To the majority, a motley collection of idle impostors and inefficient poseurs, it is a cushy assignment where they can disguise their ignorance and incompetence behind a welter of excuses. Of course convoys are attacked and ships lost, but you can bet your shirt that the warship lagging behind when the fighting starts is commanded by one of these Reservist delinquents. They brag ashore, strut at sea when it's quiet, and when the enemy appears, can be relied upon to do the wrong thing at the wrong time. In this respect the worst I have met is a French-Canadian.

He expresses dislike of Englishmen generally and is cordially hated in return by his crew. Only by a blustering bogus form of authority can he maintain any sort of discipline…

There was more, but Strong threw the cutting aside in disgust, unable to stomach any more of the ridiculous, vindictive nonsense. He thought back to the days immediately prior to leaving Liverpool when he had lectured Boland on his idleness. No, that could not be the reason; the man was much too intelligent.

Now he had it. The girl, Captain D's secretary. What was her name…? Joan something. Yes, he had stopped the Navigator taking her out one day and, if he remembered rightly, it was the one incident that had aroused Boland's temper. Yes, it was possible that when Boland wanted a woman he wanted her badly, would brook no interference. That's what had caused it, of course. On the spur of the moment, and in a flaming rage, he had written this story and sent it off before they sailed. My

God, what a bloody fool! Did he really think he could get away with it; probably relying on the paper to cover his tracks and back him up? What a mess; a stupid, unnecessary, distasteful mess. He wondered vaguely if Admiral Quigley had been informed.

He picked up the article again and read it through to the end. Amazement changed to anger, a deep anger, that a grown man should have such an incredible facility for exposing his vanity and shallowness so blatantly.

He thrashed the problem for thirty minutes, allowing his mind to clear, his resentment to die. The present Peter Boland, he thought bitterly, was so different from the author of this article that he might well be ashamed. But how could he be saved from his own stupidity? This was impossible, but somehow he had to prevent it growing into a fatal, overwhelming blunder.

A knock on the door interrupted his thoughts. 'Yes, come in.'

A messenger thrust his head quickly round the door. 'Admiral's compliments, sir. Would you report to him right away.'

'Very good.'

The head vanished and Strong stood up, frowning at the offending cutting. It did not occur to him that he should be personally resentful; that as the obvious target for Boland's mischief he should be bitterly vengeful. His only concern was how to extract the Navigator from a predicament which could wreck his career not only in the Navy for the duration, but also as a journalist.

What could he say to Quigley?

He passed through the Operations Room, glancing automatically at the huge map of the Atlantic with the models representing convoys, escorts, aircraft and single ships, waved to the staff officer on duty and saw the Admiral outside his office talking to Chief and the dockyard superintendent.

'You wanted me, sir?' he asked quietly.

'Hullo, Strong. Yes, I've got a report here from the Engineer Captain. I've been talking to Murray and the Super about it. Seems you were damn lucky to reach port. Come on in.'

Strong muttered 'See you later' to the Chief and followed the Admiral into the large, sparsely furnished office. He noticed the photographs of Quigley's wife and daughter on the desk and thought inconsequentially that Miss Quigley was not just attractive, she was lovely. Must be about twenty-four or thereabouts, and he wondered if she was at St John's. He averted his eyes guiltily.

'Now, Strong, sit down and smoke if you want to. I asked you to see me because I have to decide what to do with your officers and ship's company. It's pretty certain from this report on *Concord*'s damage that she will have to go into dry dock. Apart from all the visible damage, it seems both propeller shafts are slightly out of line. There's more like that as well.

'We can't do all that here — no facilities. I propose sending her to Boston Navy Yard under tow. That's the nearest place that can deal with her. On tow it should take no more than four or five days. You will stay in command, of course, and your Chief will have to go along. I'll send about half the ship's company; that should be enough, and the rest can go into the pool here until proper draft orders come through for key ratings.'

'When will this happen, sir?'

'When the weather clears. Say day after tomorrow — the nth.'

'What shall I do after that, sir?'

'We'll come to that later, Strong. First I want to know how you feel about your officers, excluding Chief, of course, and probably the doctor — Goodwin, isn't it? — who will have to be sent back to England straight away.'

This was not proceeding along the lines Strong had expected. His mind was still in a turmoil about Boland. There was, however, one officer on whom he could be definite.

'I don't want Lieutenant Grant, sir. In my confidential report I have had to recommend that he be given a shore job of some sort and regarded as unfit for further sea duty. I hate having to say that about anyone, sir, but I'm afraid that in this case there was no alternative.'

'What's the matter with the boy?'

'It's not his fault really. We had no action on that trip, just the hurricane. Yet at times he was frightened, horribly scared. Worse, he showed it. The crew saw him and I don't believe they could ever respect him again.'

'What about another ship? No one would know and, with a little more experience, he might grow out of it.'

'No, sir. When he first joined *Concord* I thought he would turn out all right. I was wrong. But not this time. Grant is a healthy, well-set-up chap, but inside he's scared of this war, of most things, perhaps. I believe he was a bank clerk until the Navy got him. Why not give him some operations or administrative job?'

Quigley shrugged. 'Not up to me. I'll have to send him back to the U.K. with the doctor for the appointments people to deal with. You are perfectly right, of course. He'll probably make a damn good desk-rider. What about the rest?'

'Guns and the Mid are all right, sir. I'll take them with me to Boston.'

'Yes, of course. Is that all?'

Then Strong knew that this was the Admiral's way of working round to the unpleasant business of Peter Boland.

'You mean my acting First Lieutenant, Peter Boland, sir?'

Quigley sat down behind his desk and looked hard at Strong. 'Yes, I do.'

'I have had instructions from the Admiralty about Lieutenant Boland which I intended bringing to you later, sir. Do you know about them?'

'Good Lord, yes. What do you think Admirals are for, Strong? Have you seen the man yet?'

'No, sir.'

'Good. When you do, I want two of my staff officers with you. Bloody impertinence of the man. This is one court that should cashier the blighter. Still, worst that can happen will be dismissal of ship, reduction in seniority and severe reprimand, I suppose.'

Strong squirmed in his chair. This was not what he wanted, but how could he explain to Quigley the extent to which Boland had changed and the circumstances under which the article had been written? He decided to try.

'It's not as simple as that, sir. Oh, I'm sure Boland wrote it. But I think I should tell you why first.'

Quigley listened silently while Strong outlined briefly what had happened the day he had called Boland to his cabin. He bisected Boland's character, underlined the childish pride and false sense of values which had followed too much success too early in life.

'You see, sir, Boland did really believe he had a genuine grievance. He thought this method of revenge very clever. I imagine that in the bohemian circles he was used to, it goes on all the time; back-biting, knives in the back and smart-alec manoeuvring for favours and position. That's been his life and he thought the Navy much the same. He has learned a pretty hard lesson, sir. That hurricane took something from every man aboard. It also gave something to each of us.

'No one is worse off because of the hurricane, most are better off. Boland found himself out there, sir, and didn't particularly like what he found. Since then, he has changed. There will be lapses, he can still irritate the living daylights out of people and I imagine his chasing after women won't stop just like that. But at least he has learned respect and tolerance for the other fellow. And in my book that's quite a step in the right direction.'

The central heating was making the office hot and Strong felt the sweat on his body as he struggled for unaccustomed words to express himself. At all costs he must put Boland's case in such a way that it could be dealt with summarily. He noticed that Quigley was still silent, waiting for him to finish.

'Apart from that, sir, Lieutenant Boland has proved that he has the makings of a good officer.' He took a deep breath and made a quick decision. 'In fact, sir, I'd like him to stay with me as First Lieutenant.'

The Admiral gazed at some papers on his desk. 'That's not possible and you know it. That boy will be under the Admiralty's wing for the rest of this war. You can see he's put his foot in it properly. He'll get promotion only when he is due for it, and someone will make sure he never has a responsible job again. Their Lordships don't like this sort of thing, Strong. They won't forget it easily. No, whatever happens here, he will have to go back to the U.K. and wait while the appointments people find him some harmless job where they can keep an eye on him. What's your suggestion for dealing with this?'

Strong knew the Admiral was right, but jumped at the chance to avoid a disciplinary court.

'Let me talk to him, sir. If he reacts as I think he will, then I can reprimand him. After all, I am the person he was really writing about and I should like the opportunity to deal with it personally.'

Quigley took his time about lighting a cigarette before giving his decision. 'Well, I'm not sure just who is behind this idea of taking extreme measures against the boy. I'm inclined to think someone wants to teach the *Daily Bulletin* a lesson — and that's not such a bad idea. However, we need men and spend a lot of money and time training them. All right. If you can deal with Boland yourself, go ahead. I'll square it with the Admiralty.'

He pressed a bell and a Paymaster Lieutenant, the Admiral's secretary, came in. 'We can forget the Boland affair, Waller. Commander Strong will deal with it.'

Strong smiled weakly and muttered his thanks. He rose to leave, thinking the discussion finished. Quigley waved him back to his chair. There was the suggestion of an amused grin on the Admiral's lips.

'Just how observant are you, Strong?'

The Canadian looked at him, puzzled. 'What do you mean, sir?'

Quigley let the grin spread across his face. 'Not very, eh? I've been looking at some papers on my desk. One of them concerns you — and I must say that after hearing you speak about Boland I'm damn glad. You are a good commanding officer, Commander Strong. That's twice I've said it.'

Strong glanced at the Admiral in astonishment. He took the sheet of blue paper and glanced at the filled-in printed form. It was from Royal Canadian Navy Headquarters in Ottawa, informing him that His Majesty had been pleased to confer upon him a commission as Commander. His heart jumped — a brass hat!

'Congratulations, Strong. In my view, it's long overdue.'

'Thank you, sir.'

'I've got your orders here as well. When you arrive in Boston, you are to take over command of one of the new Captain-class sloops being built there for us — *Forester* is her name, after some Yankee captain who fought us in the War of Independence.'

Strong forgot Boland in the flood of joy at being promoted and given a brand-new ship in one day. Quigley's eyes twinkled.

'Another thing, Commander. You seem to have earned yourself quite a reputation in these parts. My wife and daughter insist you come to dinner this evening. I'll be frank. My wife is looking for a strong' — he leered wickedly at the accidental pun — 'silent type to look after Scraggy — that's what we call our daughter Pat. Better watch out.'

Strong looked across at the photograph. So that was her name — Pat. Suited her, too.

'Why, sir? If you don't mind, I wouldn't dream of disappointing your wife —' he hesitated — 'or Scraggy.'

It was 5 p.m. that evening before Strong was ready to see Boland. Most of the official mail that required his personal attention had been cleared; Grant and Doc Goodwin had received their orders to return to the U.K. in a ship leaving on the 16th; Guns and Mid had been ordered to stand by *Concord* with one watch from the original crew. The rest were to have a week's leave in Halifax before dispersing to other ships. There remained the matter of Boland and a replacement First Lieutenant for the tow to Boston.

He answered a knock on the door and set his face grimly as Boland walked in with his cap hugged under his left arm. *Same scene, different place,* he thought ruefully.

'You sent for me, sir?'

Peter Boland watched Strong pretend to sort out letters on his table, noticed that the polite formality of their relationship during the last few days of the hurricane was missing. He had developed respect for his commanding officer, a respect that was tinged with admiration; for his earlier behaviour and attitude he felt nothing but disgust. That he had been inadequate to meet the personal challenge of the switch from arrogant self-assertion in Fleet Street to disciplined authority and obedience in the Service was self-evident.

He had plunged into the business of making amends with relief that he had found out about himself in time.

Since Masefield's death he had felt that the only mirror which could reflect a change for the better would be approval. This would be the measure of success, the accolade of his personal triumph of self-vindication.

And although Strong treated him reasonably, there were no signs of the confidence, faith and trust he had shown in his relationship with John Masefield. Like most reformed people, Boland could not understand that it was all too recent, that it is not enough just to reform; there has to be evidence that the reformation is not the temporary offshoot of a guilt complex. He could not understand that although Strong might notice the change, encourage it and accept the motives behind it, he would for a long time keep a wary eye open for lapses.

So when Boland stood before his Captain there was simmering disappointment and the frustrating knowledge that although he might have assumed Masefield's duties he still had a long way to travel before he could lay claim to the mantle.

The hurricane, his promotion and the loss of Masefield had invested Strong with a more assured, confident authority. His impersonal voice reached out to slap at Boland.

'Before we sailed from Liverpool, did you write an article for the *Daily Bulletin*?'

My God, how the hell had he found out about that? Boland had hoped that time and distance would protect him from the storm of protest that would be bound to follow. He had regretted every word of it from the beginning of the trip but had salved his conscience with the soothing thought that it could do no real harm to Strong.

'Yes, sir.' There was just the faintest hint of misery in the admission.

Strong handed the cutting across to him. 'Is this it?

Boland glanced at the opening paragraph and thought that from a professional standpoint the paper had given him a damn good show. *Worse luck*, he thought wryly.

'Yes, sir.'

'Right, Mister Boland. Now, will you explain why you wrote it?'

'I must have been mad, sir. I realize now how stupid I was. I have always hated regimentation, sir, and I think perhaps my previous attitude to the Navy and naval officers was a refusal to fit into the mould, perhaps an adolescent desire to stand out different, to be the centre of attraction, to show a worldly superiority that was really just a sham.'

His voice had acquired a bitter edge; every word was a self-inflicted wound. He breathed heavily and continued, 'To say I'm sorry seems so inadequate now, sir, and I hope that you of all people will see how true that is. Do you believe that, sir?'

'I can see you are trying,' Strong replied noncommittally.

'There is no trying about it.' Boland bent down towards Strong, desperately anxious that he should be understood. 'I have changed. Keep me with you as First Lieutenant or Navigator of your next ship, sir, and I'll prove it.'

'You have no rights in this matter, Mister Boland. In particular, no right to request anything of me.' Strong was being deliberately cold. The words washed over Boland with the numbing effect of iced water. For the first time he seemed to see through the fog of his own arrogance what would have been clear to anyone else — that he was in serious trouble. He stared hard at Strong and saw no flicker of friendliness, no understanding, no tolerance or indulgence.

'What is going to happen about it, sir?' he said stiffly. He was standing erect with the same air of repressed indignation, thought Strong, which he had shown that day in Liverpool. When would the man learn that he could not misuse people one minute and expect them to rush at him with outstretched helping hands the next?

'You don't really know just how serious this is, do you, Mister Boland? I'll tell you.' To Boland, the Captain was looking almost baleful. 'First you committed a serious breach of King's Regulations. You must know it is not permitted for you to write articles without Admiralty approval. Next you committed the crime of evading the censorship regulations — and of all people you are well aware that stories concerning the Service in wartime must pass through the censor. Next, by the very act of writing this sort of muck, you are guilty of conduct prejudicial to the discipline and efficiency of the Navy. And, perhaps worst of all, you have provided the enemy with invaluable propaganda. In simple terms — you have given active assistance to the enemy.'

He paused to watch the effect on the young officer, noting with satisfaction the pale, set face.

'The penalty for any one of those crimes is a court martial, Mister Boland. And if you were to be found guilty on all counts you might well be faced with dismissal from the Service, certainly from your ship. Now do you understand?'

Boland's mouth opened as he struggled for words. They exploded in a stream.

'That's not true. A stupid article that no one with any sense would believe anyway?' Anger thrust itself into his voice.

Strong allowed Boland to control himself.

'You are entitled to your own opinions; you are not entitled to speak to your commanding officer like that. Fortunately for you, the Admiralty have left the question of how you should be dealt with to my discretion.' This slight distortion of the truth came glibly enough, but there were stirrings of doubt about the wisdom of what he was doing. Perhaps this is all wrong, he argued to himself. Boland might well revert to type and get himself into far worse trouble later.

'I know what really inspired that article — it was spite because I interfered with some affair you were having with a Wren. For this reason, I am not going to recommend a court martial. Instead, I want your word that you will not write another article, unless with Admiralty approval, while you are wearing uniform.

'I don't want you serving with me again. You will be sent back to the U.K. for another appointment.'

Boland interrupted in alarm. Only Strong's respect really mattered. If he could not serve under Strong, his efforts to prove himself would be cheated of the final triumph.

'No, sir. I want to serve under you.'

'No. Frankly, I don't want you anywhere near a ship of mine. I want that promise and I have another job — call it a penalty, if you like — for you in London. I am not sure what went wrong with John Masefield's marriage, but one of us should see her and explain how John died. I can think of no one more suitable for that duty than you.'

Boland was astounded.

'My God, no. I made John's life hell. I must have twisted a knife in him every time I mentioned Sonia. I couldn't go near her without feeling as guilty of his death as you think I am. I won't do it, sir. She'll blame me too.'

'Yes, you will, Boland. It's the least you can do, and Sonia must be told by one of us, one of his colleagues. We owe her that. You can go now.'

The two officers stared hard at each other, fury from one, cold implacability in the other. As Boland left the room, he wondered how long it would be before Strong requested his court martial.

Two days passed with hardly a word passing between Strong and Boland. Then *Concord* sailed for Boston with the tug *Mormon.* Boland sat in the wardroom ashore struggling to resolve the emotional conflict which had consumed him since his outburst. He wanted to hate Strong, but he knew without being able to recognize it that some ingredient of the quarrel was eluding him.

The Admiral's Secretary sat beside him, ordered a drink and said, 'Thought you would be down at the docks seeing your ship off. Must be a hell of a good chap to serve with, that Strong.'

Boland glanced at him in annoyance. 'How wrong you are. Bloody man's impossible. Thank God he's out of the way.'

The Secretary answered curiously, 'But I thought you got on well with him. He seemed to like you all right.'

'Don't be so damn silly,' Boland said with a humourless smile. 'What on earth gave you that idea? Why, he tried to think up some stupid excuses to court-martial me a couple of days ago. Man's mad.'

'Look, my dear chap.' The other officer spoke seriously. 'It's about time you got a few things straight. We all know about that silly article, but only I know he stopped you getting into really bad trouble. You may not know it but the Admiralty instructed him to report you to the Admiral — and Quigley was all for throwing the book at you. Louis Strong talked him out of it, Boland. Said the reason you wrote it concerned him and therefore he would prefer to deal with it himself. Strictly, it was already out of his hands. But for some reason the Admiral agreed to square matters with the Admiralty. Strong saved your neck, Boland, and frankly, I'm wondering why.'

As Boland listened, an expression of peace settled over his face. At the end, he was smiling.

'So that's what happened.'

11

Peter Boland sat in a Fleet Street bar waiting for the News Editor of the *Daily Bulletin* to arrive for his customary morning drink — a meticulous fragment of routine which had taken place at the same time each day for twenty years. He was content, thinking affectionately of Strong. He had learned to understand Masefield's worship for the Canadian. That morning he had called at the office of the Admiral Commanding, Reserves, for an interview with Commander Manners in the appointments department.

'I sent for you, Boland,' said Manners affably, 'because you can have one of two things — a Number One's job in a corvette or command of an asdic trawler. Which do you want?'

'The corvette as First Lieutenant.' He knew this was what Strong would have wanted him to choose. He was not ready yet for command of a rowing boat.

The next step of the morning had been simple. A taxi from St James's to Fleet Street, a planned encounter with his former News Editor.

There he was now, the lined, eager, ageless face pushing through to the bar and lighting with pleased recognition of a colleague back from the wars. Boland ordered the drinks and, when the welcome had died, said with quiet finality, 'Here's a note for the chief. It's my resignation from the paper, old boy. No more articles, no more ambition, no more blue-eyed-boy assignments. I've just joined the Navy.'

The News Editor looked at him thoughtfully. 'Yes, Peter, I think you have joined the Navy at last. I think you've just grown up too.'

'I shall know about that this evening,' Boland replied. 'A duty call to make which in a peculiar way might also be a form of atonement.'

That evening he telephoned Sonia Masefield. She answered gaily.

'Hullo, Peter darling. Where are you? In town, I hope.'

'Yes, Sonia. Look, can we meet this evening? I have something to tell you.'

Her voice changed — hardened with an undercurrent of desperation.

'It's about John, isn't it? I got the telegram a few days ago. You want to tell me how it happened.'

'Yes. In a way. But there's more. What time shall we meet?'

The gaiety returned, forced and subdued.

'Eleven o'clock, Peter. After the show. You come here. I've got some friends coming round for drinks.'

'But I want to see you alone, Sonia. This is serious.'

'Nonsense, darling. I'm a lonely widow now and I need comforting. See you at eleven.'

He replaced the receiver, puzzled. He had expected tears, hysterics, perhaps. Although it was obvious the Masefields had quarrelled, they had always seemed very much in love. Everyone knew that Masefield had adored her — and took it for granted that she had adored him.

He dismissed the nagging pricks of conscience and rehearsed for the hundredth time how he would explain the tragedy and his own part in it. No beating about the bush, he had decided, just the truth. But he recoiled from the scene that would surely follow, the accusing eyes revealing her conviction that he, Boland, should be dead, not John Masefield.

It was nearly half past eleven when he arrived at St Ives Court, took a lift to the fourth floor and knocked on the door of Flat 401. No one answered, although the sounds of activity inside were plain. He knocked again and rang the bell.

The door opened and a dark young woman, petite, pretty and slightly drunk, peered up at him with laughing, admiring eyes.

'What do you want, sailor? A bed for the night?' She wagged a finger at him. 'Naughty sailor, coming here for a bed. This isn't a brothel, you know, though…' Her voice trailed off as she gave him a lingering look. 'No, you'd better go down Piccadilly, sailor. This isn't for you.'

Grinning slightly, he pushed his way in. 'Yes, I know what you mean, but I'm invited. This is Mrs Masefield's flat?'

'Oh, goody.' She was drunker than he had thought. 'I saw you first, you're mine. Come in and I'll buy you a drink. Then we can go over into the corner there and get acquainted, Lootenant … oh, hell! Sonia's there; she always bags the corner settee. Come on, Lootenant, this way to the bar…'

With a sense of complete unreality, Boland grabbed her arm and whispered urgently, 'Who's that man with Mrs Masefield — the one kissing her?'

The young woman giggled. 'That's her current lover, sailor boy. Why? You jealous?'

Her darkly provocative face looked up at him mockingly. Then her expression changed and she screwed up her eyes in an effort to concentrate. Her voice was a blurred, anxious squeak.

'My God, Sonia once mentioned she had a husband in the Navy. You him?'

Boland turned away from the scene in the corner with a feeling of cynical disgust. He remembered Masefield the First Lieutenant welding a hundred and fifty men into an efficient fighting unit; Masefield, that asdic specialist, assuming so damned ruthlessly the role of rapier to Strong's sword in so many U-boat-busting doubles; Masefield, who had defied the worst hurricane on record in a frail motor boat to rescue a handful of *Firefly*'s crew.

And with these flickering pictures from the past came hateful memories of his own brutal insinuations and taunts, so accurately and unknowingly aimed to torment a man carrying not only the burden of duty but that of a faithless wife.

The woman's voice broke in on his thoughts. 'I hope you're not, sailor boy, 'cos you're too nice for that sex-crazy tart. I like you; come on, let's have a drink.'

His eyes explored her without insult but as though for the first time. 'No, I'm not her husband. And no drink. I want to get out of here as fast as I can. Goodbye.'

He turned towards the door, and she hurried after him with a cry: 'Hey, wait for me.' He waited while she searched for coat and handbag. And when the door had closed behind them the pattern of the hurricane and its aftermath at St John's fell neatly into place.

'One of us should see her and explain how John died,' Strong had said. 'I can think of no one more suitable for this duty than you.'

A NOTE TO THE READER

If you have enjoyed this novel enough to leave a review on **Amazon** and **Goodreads**, then we would be truly grateful.

Sapere Books

SAPERE
BOOKS

Printed in Great Britain
by Amazon